WHEN THE SKY FELL GOLD

SOMETIMES MIRACLES COME WEARING SCARS

SHIV BHOWMIK

To Maa and Baba,

who held me when the world let go,

who heard the words I never said,

and believed in me even when I forgot how to.

You've been the quiet strength behind every broken moment.

the hands that lifted me, again and again...

without complaint, without pause.

In your love, I found my footing.

In your patience, I found my voice.

And in your unwavering faith,

I found the courage to write this story.

This book breathes because of you.

With all my heart,

—Shiv

Contents

Contents

Acknowledgements

This book could not have been written without the shadows that shaped it, the people who stood beside me, and the love that lifted me through the quiet wars of writing.

To Maa and Baba... your strength is the spine of this story. You held me up when I doubted myself. You saw light in the darkest chapters and reminded me, always, that stories heal. This book belongs to you before it belongs to anyone else.

To the quiet believers... the ones who asked, "How's the writing going?" without expecting a polished answer, who read drafts, offered kind truths, and reminded me to keep going... thank you.

To the city of Mumbai... its chaos, its resilience, its broken beauty... you are a character in this story as much as any of them. You taught me that even in the mess, there is magic.

To the readers... those who have ever felt unseen, unheard, or unworthy—I hope you find something here that whispers back to you, "You matter."

And finally, to the voice inside me that said, "This story needs to be told," I'm glad I listened.

With gratitude,
Shiv Bhowmik

Foreword

When the Sky Fell Gold is more than just a story... it's an echo of survival, a quiet scream from the margins, and a raw chronicle of human fragility that refuses to surrender.

Shiv Bhowmik has crafted a modern urban fable set in the pulsing heart of Mumbai, where the ordinary becomes extraordinary and the broken become whole. The narrative unfolds not in polished homes or perfect lives, but in chawls, rooftop terraces, and rain-slick alleyways. Here, the gold doesn't glitter in banks... it falls from the sky, violently and without warning, into the hands of those most overlooked.

As a reader, you won't merely witness the events that unfold... you'll feel them tremble under your skin. You'll bleed with Rahul, rage with Sujata, crawl beside Dev, and resist with Chung. And somewhere in their journey, you might just find picces of your own story stitchcd bctween the silences.

This novel reminds us that sometimes, survival is the purest form of rebellion.

And sometimes, miracles come wearing scars.

Preface

There's a moment—a sharp, unbearable moment—where everything feels like it's falling apart.

When hope feels too heavy to carry.

When silence feels louder than the sky itself.

When the Sky Fell Gold was born from that moment.

This story is not about superheroes or perfect lives.

It's about people who have been broken, bent, and battered by life—and yet still dared to believe that something better could be waiting beyond the next fall.

It's about survival, not as an act of strength, but as an act of stubborn, beautiful hope.

Rahul, Sujata, Chung, and Dev are fictional—but their struggles are real.

They represent all of us who have been laughed at, underestimated, hurt, or forgotten—and still found a way to keep dreaming.

This book is a reminder that sometimes, the sky doesn't fall to punish us.

It falls to show us that even in the ashes of broken things, there can be gold.

There can be new beginnings.

Thank you for stepping into this journey.

Thank you for believing—even for just a few pages—that broken doesn't mean defeated.

— **Shiv Bhowmik**

Prologue

The city of Mumbai never truly slept, but on this night, it tossed and turned in a fever dream of quiet desperation. Through the paper-thin walls of a thousand chawls, the city's private agonies bled into one another—a woman's sharp, hissing argument over unpaid bills became the percussive backdrop to a man's broken, muttered prayers to a god who had long stopped listening. In a room nearby, a child's stomach ached with a hunger so profound that his sleeping mind could only conjure the phantom taste of a feast he would never eat. These were the small, individual heartbreaks that formed the city's restless, collective soul. Mumbai did not pause for such things; its indifferent hum was the sound of a great machine grinding them all down into silence.

The wind howled over the lip of the unfinished bridge, a raw, abrasive sound that scraped at the night. It whipped Rahul's cheap office shirt against his skin, the cold fabric a flimsy barrier against the vast, empty darkness. Below, the city was a distant, silent smear of lights, their reflections glittering like false diamonds on the black water. His old motorbike idled behind him, its engine a low, anxious tremor that vibrated up from the soles of his worn-out shoes and into his bones—the last feeling in a world that had otherwise gone numb. Beneath his feet, the bridge gave a rhythmic, hollow thrum-thud as a distant truck hit a loose expansion joint. It was a metallic heartbeat for a structure that led nowhere.

He gripped his helmet, his knuckles aching from the pressure, the smooth plastic a useless, hollow thing in his hands. This wasn't a sudden decision. It was the final, quiet exhale at the end of a lifetime of holding his breath. He could almost feel the weight of every compromise he had ever made, every swallowed insult that had left the faint taste of acid at the back of his throat. He remembered the faint smirk on his boss's face just yesterday, the way he had forced a nod and a smile while a part of him withered inside. It was the slow, steady erosion of a man. The hollowness in his chest was a physical ache now, a vacant space where a self used to be. He was a ghost haunting the edges of his own life. The realization wasn't tragic. It was just true. And he was tired. Enough.

A few miles away, loose grit scraped under the cheap plastic of Sujata's heels as she stood at the edge of a crumbling rooftop. Her knuckles were bone-white where she gripped the cold, rusted railing, the corroded metal a final, flimsy connection to the world. A sudden gust of wind pushed at her back, a physical, insistent pressure urging her forward. Below, the city's lights swam and blurred into a dizzying, indifferent sea. The relentless noise of Mumbai was gone up here, but it had been replaced by a far more deafening roar inside her own head. It was a chaotic chorus of her failures: the landlord's sneering voice reminding her the rent was due, the doctor's carefully worded pity, and the wet, slurred whispers of the men at the bar, their eyes stripping her down to the sum of her debts. It was an endless, looping soundtrack of compromise and shame. She mouthed her sister's name, a silent, desperate apology that the wind immediately tore from her lips. Then, with a final, shuddering exhale, she closed her eyes, not in search of peace, but in a desperate, frantic plea for the noise to finally, finally stop.

Across the city, the cold rain pattering on her balcony did nothing to wash away the thick, coppery smell of blood that filled her small apartment. Chung stumbled out into the night air, her lungs burning, each breath catching in a ragged, rattling sob that felt like swallowing glass. She couldn't escape the image seared into her mind: the stranger's body, a broken, sprawling silhouette draped over the wreckage of her coffee table, the city's indifferent lights framing his unnatural stillness. A wet, sticky warmth was soaking through her sock, a sickening reminder of the fight. A wave of nausea, hot and acidic, rose in her throat. Her life had been a slow, painstaking climb up a sheer cliff face, each handhold a small, hard-won victory. Now, in the space of a few terrifying minutes, she had lost her grip, and the entire fragile structure of the self she had built was plummeting into the abyss.

Near a garbage-choked lane, Dev's world shrank to the cold, gritty asphalt pressed against his cheek. He tried to push himself up, but a nauseating, grinding pain flared in his leg, a white-hot spike of agony that stole his breath and left him gasping. The thieves' laughter was a fading, cruel echo in the night. He coughed, a wet, rattling sound, and tasted a vile mixture of his own coppery blood and the oily filth of the street. It was the taste of abject failure. The taste of a thousand silent sacrifices that had amounted to nothing. The taste of being utterly, completely alone. No one was coming for him. The thought landed not as a shock, but as a quiet, final confirmation of a truth he had always known. He stopped fighting. He let his body go limp on the wet ground, the cold rain plastering his thin shirt to his skin as he stared up at the empty, starless sky. For the first time in his life, he wasn't wishing or hoping or praying. He was simply done. He closed his eyes and, with a final, shuddering exhale, let go.

The night pressed down, a final, suffocating weight. Across the city, in four separate pockets of darkness, four souls had reached their final exhalation. The city had become a tomb, and they were ready, in their own silent ways, to be interred.

And then the heavens tore open.

It began not with a sound, but with a silent, violent wound in the fabric of the night. A fissure of impossible, golden-blue light ripped across the sky, spilling a brilliance so absolute it felt like a physical pressure against their skin. This was not daylight; it was something older, something holy and terrifying. It bleached the world of color and shadow, exposing the city's grime—the rust on the railing, the cracks in the concrete, the filth in the gutter—with a stark, divine clarity.

On the bridge, Rahul's body reacted before his mind could, recoiling from the edge he had just been seeking. On the rooftop, the internal scream in Sujata's mind was violently silenced by the external brilliance, her eyes flying open in her tear-streaked face. On the balcony, Chung's panic was instantly replaced by an artist's stunned awe at a color she had never known existed. And in the gutter, Dev, with a grunt of pain, turned his head from the asphalt for the first time, his gaze dragged upward from his own miserable reflection.

Then came the sound. It was not a roar that traveled through the air but a deep, concussive boom that punched up through the soles of their feet, a physical blow to the chest that seemed to shake the very foundations of the city. It was the sound of something ancient and vast breaking free.

Following the sound, a single, burning star emerged from the tear in the sky. It fell, not with the gentle grace of a meteor, but with the violent purpose of a spear, cleaving a path through the clouds faster than a human prayer could be formed. It left a shimmering, incandescent scar against the darkness as it plunged toward the forgotten wastelands at the city's edge, a promise of either a spectacular end or a terrifying new beginning. None of them knew it yet, but the sky had not broken to crush them. It had broken to find them. And in the fire of its impact, a new world was waiting to be born.

CHAPTER ONE

Rahul's Fall

The office air was thick with the ghost of burnt tea from a long-abandoned pot, a smell that had become synonymous with wasted ambition. It mingled with the scent of dusty files and the faint, chemical tang of cheap cleaning fluid, creating an atmosphere of quiet, permanent decay. Rahul sat hunched at his desk, his shoulders molded into the permanent slump of a man who had given up years ago. On the screen before him, an Excel sheet shimmered, and a single cursor blinked with a tiny, relentless rhythm. It was a digital heartbeat for a room that had no soul, a bored child demanding his attention. The cursor blinked, but Rahul's mind did not. The weariness he felt had long ago seeped past his muscles and into his bones, calcifying there into something heavier and more immovable than simple fatigue.

He watched the wall clock tick past 7:04 p.m. Everyone else had fled, leaving a silence that felt heavy and expectant. Everyone except her.

"Rahul! " The barked command from the glass cabin was sharp enough to make him flinch. "In here. Now."

He grabbed his notepad, a useless shield, and made the long walk across the empty office, feeling like a schoolboy summoned to the headmistress's office for a caning. Meghna Shroff didn't look up when he entered. The only sound was the aggressive, high-pitched click of her long nails on the keyboard. "Explain this," she said, her voice cold as steel as she rotated her monitor. A section of a spreadsheet was highlighted in a furious, bleeding red.

"It's a vendor quote variance," Rahul said, his voice sounding thin and reedy in the sterile room. "I escalated it in the group—"

"You escalated it *in the chat?*" She finally looked up, her kohl-lined eyes narrowing with theatrical disbelief. "Oh, Rahul. You're adorable."

His throat went dry. She rose from her chair then, a slow, deliberate movement, and began to circle him like a predator sizing up its prey. An aggressive cloud of her expensive perfume enveloped him, making it hard to breathe. "Do you have any idea why you still work here?" she asked, her voice a soft, cruel purr.

He stiffened, bracing himself. This was her favorite performance. "I..."

"It's not because you're good at your job," she cut in smoothly. "It's because you are a sad, fifty-year-old man in cheap shoes who reeks of desperation. You are a piece of reliable, depressing furniture."

A poorly suppressed snicker echoed from the doorway, which she had deliberately left ajar. Rahul's gaze darted over. Two interns were watching, their faces alight with cruel amusement. One of them had his phone up, recording. A hot, violent wave of shame washed over Rahul, flooding his face and ears. He could feel the cold, black lens of the camera on him, a single, unblinking eye broadcasting his humiliation to the world.

Meghna saw his gaze, and her smile widened. "You have no ambition," she continued, her voice rising for the benefit of her audience. "You sulk around like a kicked dog. Honestly, if you can't even afford the commute, go sell pani puri." The words were not just insults; they were a public vivisection. He clenched his notepad so hard his knuckles ached, the spiral wire biting into his palm.

"Now get out," she said, dismissing him with a flick of her wrist. "And think long and hard about whether you even deserve to come back tomorrow." Her phone buzzed, and she glanced at it, a genuine, unrelated smile touching her lips for a moment. Then her eyes found his again, and her voice dropped to a venomous whisper. "And try not to waste so much of my oxygen."

He walked out into the echoing cavern of the basement parking lot. The harsh, buzzing fluorescent tubes above bleached all the color from his skin, making him look as sallow and lifeless as he felt. Meghna's final, cruel words—*waste so much of my oxygen*—seemed to hang in the damp, heavy air, leaving the taste of ash and failure in his mouth. The security guard, whose face was as familiar and anonymous as the concrete pillars, gave him a quiet, pitying nod. It was a look that said, *I see you, brother. I see your defeat.* It was worse than any insult.

He swung a leg over his aging Honda Shine. The first turn of the key produced a weak, clicking sound. The second, a pathetic, gurgling cough. On the third, the engine finally caught, a rattling, unhealthy shudder that was the perfect mechanical expression of his own soul. He pulled out onto the deserted street, and as the empty business park fell away behind him, the memories closed in.

The thought of Meghna's proposition from last week returned, a slick and oily memory that made his skin crawl.

Her words about "synergy" and "after-hours team building" had been a thin, corporate veil over a brutish demand. Become her plaything and her stress reliever, and a promotion would follow. His quiet, firm refusal had signed his death warrant. Today's public execution was simply the sentence being carried out.

He twisted the accelerator, not gently, but with a surge of self-loathing. The bike lurched, its small engine whining in protest. The painted white lines on the asphalt began to flicker in his headlights, a hypnotic, strobing rhythm pulling him forward. Meghna's voice, dripping with condescending pity, started to echo in his helmet, weaving itself into another, older voice. His ex-wife's. He could see the fury in her eyes and could hear the sharp, percussive thud of his own shoe hitting the wall beside his head. *"You smell like failure, Rahul! "* The shriek was as clear now as it had been a decade ago.

He pushed the bike faster, urging more speed from the protesting engine. The wind roared in his ears, a physical wall of sound, but it wasn't enough to drown out the chorus of his humiliations. The landlord's voice, polite but laced with steel: *"The first of the month, Rahul-ji, as we agreed."* The shopkeeper's silent, pitying gaze as he counted out coins for the cheapest brand of soap. He was a man defined not by what he had, but by what he lacked. What was even left to salvage? A collection of worn-out shirts, overdue bills, and fresh, stinging shame.

Ahead, the unfinished bridge cut a stark, black line against the starless sky. It wasn't just a piece of road. It was an end. A full stop. An invitation. A cold, serene calm settled over him. This was the answer. He pressed his hand down, twisting the accelerator as far as it would go. The engine screamed, and the concrete barrier at the road's end grew from a line to a shape, from a shape to a wall. It was a promise of absolute, final silence. For a single, rebellious heartbeat, some deep, animal instinct screamed at him to brake, to swerve, to live. But the man at the controls was too tired to listen. A roar of pure, soul-crushing exhaustion ripped through his mind, a single, definitive word. *Enough.* He kept his eyes wide open, ready to greet the end.

And then, the sky shattered.

It wasn't a light; it was a physical presence. A violent, silent tear in the fabric of the night that bleached the world in an impossible golden-blue glare. Every crack in the asphalt, every rusted bolt on the bridge railing, was thrown into stark, blinding relief.

Instinct, not thought, made him slam on the brakes. The rear tire locked, and the bike skidded sideways in a screech of tortured rubber. His body was thrown forward, the helmet strap biting viciously into his neck as he fought to keep from flying over the handlebars. He wrestled the bike to a shuddering halt, his heart kicking against his ribs.

He looked up, gasping. Above him, a burning object tore through the atmosphere, not just falling but cleaving a path through the night. It trailed sparks of liquid fire, and the air itself seemed to scream in its wake. Moments later, a deep, guttural boom rolled across the landscape, a tremor vibrating up through the bike's frame and into his bones. Far in the distance, toward the abandoned textile estates, a plume of smoke and orange light began to curl into the sky.

Rahul could only stare, his chest heaving, the earlier despair vaporized by sheer, terrifying awe. "What the hell..." he breathed into the sudden, ringing silence.

The world outside was quiet again, but inside him, a tectonic shift had occurred. The man who had ridden onto this bridge seeking an end was gone. He had stared into the abyss, and something infinitely larger and stranger had stared back. He didn't ride home. He didn't ride to the office. With hands that still trembled, he turned the bike around and aimed it toward the column of smoke. He wasn't sure why, except that death had been denied to him by a falling star, and he felt a sudden, inexplicable need to see what the universe had sent in its place.

CHAPTER TWO

SUJATA'S COLLAPSE

The bass wasn't just a sound; it was a concussion. A relentless, physical thudding that traveled up through the soles of Sujata's cheap heels, through her aching legs, and settled deep in her teeth. With every beat, the sticky, unwashed glasses on the shelf behind her rattled a miserable chorus. She tugged at the hem of the tight red dress—a mistake, she knew now—the cheap, synthetic fabric clinging and riding up her thighs. She forced the muscles in her face to hold a smile, a brittle, hollow expression she had practiced in a cracked mirror until it became a mask. Each time she leaned over the bar, a dull, grinding ache flared in her lower back, a counterpoint to the sharp, stabbing pain in the arches of her feet. The air itself was a suffocating cocktail of spilled rum, stale sweat, and the cloying, sweet smell of desperation.

"Another round, sweetheart!"

The voice was a thick, liquor-soaked bark. A man in his mid-forties slammed a wad of crumpled, damp bills onto the counter. His wedding ring was a flash of dull gold under the lurid neon light. Sujata's mask-like smile didn't waver.

She gave a small, mechanical nod and reached for a chipped glass, her entire focus narrowing to the task of pouring two fingers of whiskey. She did not look at his face. She did not follow his gaze as it lingered on her chest. This was the work: the active, exhausting process of pretending. Pretending she didn't feel the oily curl of disgust in her stomach. Pretending her heart didn't seize with a jolt of pure animal fear every time her phone vibrated with a summons from her boss. Most of all, pretending that she was not slowly, transaction by transaction, turning into a ghost. She had to. Every forced smile, every swallowed insult, was another brick in the wall she was building around the one clean, pure thing left in her world. Her reason. Her prayer.

Anaya.

The phone buzzed against the wooden shelf, the sharp, insistent vibration cutting through the bar's dull roar. It wasn't just a notification; it was a summons. From Vikrant. The devil himself. The vibration was a physical jolt, a miniature earthquake that sent a chill skittering up her spine and transported her instantly back seven months. Back to the low, indifferent hum of the ICU, the sterile scent of antiseptic, and her sister's final, ragged words clinging to the air like smoke: *"Sujata... please... take care of her."* Hope had a price. Sujata was still paying.

Wiping her damp, trembling hands on a bar towel, she stepped into the claustrophobic confines of the stockroom. The message was simple, almost playful: *Check your WhatsApp.* Frowning, she switched apps. A video file. Her thumb hovered over it for a second, a flicker of premonition making her hesitate. She tapped it. The world dissolved.

The blood drained from her face, leaving her skin feeling cold and tight. The small screen filled with a grainy, dark image of these very shelves, this very room. And her. Half-naked, her face flushed and twisted in a parody of pleasure. His face was a strategic, cowardly blur. Hers was in perfect, damning focus. The sound was a muffled, ugly recording of her own voice. A wave of hot, acidic nausea rose in her throat. *No.* It was a silent scream in her mind. *He promised.* The ugly, necessary transactions she had endured for Anaya's medical bills were supposed to have been secret. No photos. No videos. No evidence. *He had promised.*

Her hands were shaking so violently she could barely hold the phone. She tried to call him, her thumb jabbing at the screen. Voicemail. A moment later, the stockroom door creaked open. Vikrant sauntered in, cloaked in a cloud of his cheap, overpowering cologne.

"Hey, sexy," he drawled, the smug smirk on his face confirming the depth of his betrayal.

"You filmed it?" The words were a strangled, choked whisper, barely audible.

He shrugged, a gesture of such casual cruelty it made her stomach clench. "Relax," he said, enjoying her terror. "It's just our little secret. For now."

"What do you want?" she asked, her voice a thin, trembling thread.

"Simple." He leaned against the doorframe, a lazy predator who knew his prey was trapped. "Twenty-five lakhs. Cash. I delete everything."

The number was so absurd, so impossible, it was like being struck by lightning. "Twenty-five lakhs?" she gasped. "Vikrant, you know I don't have twenty-five thousand!"

"That sounds like a you problem," he said, blowing a lazy stream of smoke toward the ceiling. "You've got one day to figure it out. Or the whole internet gets a free show."

Tears of pure, helpless rage blurred her vision. "You are a monster."

He stepped closer, his voice dropping to a low, conspiratorial whisper that made her skin crawl. "You knew what you were getting into. Don't play the innocent little victim now."

That was it. The condescension in his voice, the utter lack of remorse—it was a spark hitting gasoline. The terror and the shame and the helplessness finally ignited into a single, clarifying blast of pure, white-hot rage. Before her mind could even process the decision, her body acted. She shoved him, not with a push, but with a full-bodied, explosive heave. Surprise flashed in his eyes as he stumbled backward, his arms flailing. He crashed hard against a metal shelving unit, and the sickening crack of his head hitting the steel edge echoed in the tiny room. For one long, silent, horrifying heartbeat, he lay still. *Oh god, did I kill him?* Then he groaned, a low, animal sound, and clutched his head. A dark trickle of blood snaked down from his temple. He was alive. And he was furious.

He struggled to his feet, his face a mask of pure, contorted rage. "You're fired!" he roared. "Get the hell out of my sight! And you find my money, you hear me? You find my money, or by this time tomorrow, you'll be the most famous whore in Mumbai!"

The moments after Vikrant's roar were a smear of bleeding neon and blurred motion. The words—*Fired. Broke. "Blackmailed"—they were* not just words; they were a death sentence, repeating over and over in her mind. The thought of Anaya seeing that video, of the shame in her innocent eyes, was a shard of ice twisting in her gut. She walked, her cheap heels clacking on the empty sidewalk, a frantic, desperate rhythm counting down her final minutes.

The city's last gasps—a drunken argument, a dog tearing at garbage—were sounds from a world she had already left. Ahead, the abandoned textile mill apartments clawed at the night sky, a skeleton of rust and concrete. Five floors of perfect, silent oblivion. It was calling to her.

At the entrance, she kicked off her heels. The first one landed with a soft clatter. The second, she didn't even hear. They were the last prayer of a life she was now shedding. Barefoot, she stepped into the darkness of the stairwell. The air was cold and damp, smelling of decay. She climbed. Each cracked concrete step was cold against her numb feet. The echo of her own footfalls was a hollow, lonely drumbeat following her up, a funeral procession of one. One floor. Two. Three. With each level, the sounds of the city grew fainter, and the world she was leaving became more distant. Four. Five.

The terrace door groaned open on rusted hinges, and the wind hit her like a physical blow. It was a wild, fierce thing up here, tearing at her dress, whipping her hair into a stinging frenzy across her face. The whole of Mumbai spread out below her, a silent, glittering carpet of a million lives that felt utterly alien. The city's relentless hum was gone, replaced by the raw, lonely howl of the wind. Up here, it was finally quiet enough to die.

She walked to the ledge, the rough concrete scraping her bare feet. The drop was a dizzying, terrifying pull. She closed her eyes, the wind a cold shock on her tear-streaked face, and whispered a final, broken apology to her sister, to Anaya, and to the woman she had so spectacularly failed to become. She lifted her foot, her body already beginning to tilt forward into the vast, empty nothingness.

And in that final, silent heartbeat, a memory didn't just flash—it ambushed her. It was a full-sensory assault: the sudden, phantom smell of cheap chocolate, the sound of a tiny, wheezing gasp of pure joy, and the vivid image of Anaya's small arms reaching for her. *"Love you, Aunty Su!* "The memory was so powerful, so real, it was a physical jolt. Her foot, already poised over the abyss, wavered, a single, involuntary tremor of love fighting against the pull of oblivion.

And then the sky exploded.

A silent, impossible wave of light tore the heavens apart, smearing the darkness with violent, living streaks of gold and electric blue. The air itself seemed to crackle and thrum with an energy that made the hairs on her arms stand on end. The concrete beneath her feet trembled, and a deep, concussive boom rolled across the city, a bass note so profound it vibrated not in her ears but in her bones. She screamed, a strangled, involuntary sound, and staggered backward from the ledge, her hands flying to her face.

In the far distance, over the old mills, a plume of smoke began to rise against the scarred sky. Her heart still hammered against her ribs, but the slow, hopeless rhythm of surrender was gone, replaced by a wild, terrifying, and thunderous drumbeat of pure awe. She had come here seeking an ending. The universe, it seemed, had other, more violent plans.

CHAPTER THREE

Chung's Fight

The cheap, poorly stretched canvas ripped under the pressure of her brush. Chung let out a soft curse, but her hand didn't stop moving. With a practiced, cynical precision, she loaded her brush with a thick dab of imitation cobalt blue and worked the tear into the swirling, violent texture of a Van Gogh petal. She was an expert at turning flaws into features, at hiding imperfections until they looked like intentional acts of art. It was a skill she had learned long before she ever picked up a paintbrush.

Tonight's commission was a 70% passable forgery of *Irises*, good enough to fetch eight hundred rupees from the street vendor she supplied near the Gateway. A thousand, if she was lucky and the tourist who bought it was drunk enough on holiday spirit not to look too closely. The sharp, chemical bite of turpentine filled her small studio. It was a smell that other artists might associate with creation and hope. For Chung, it was simply the smell of another month's rent.

Her studio was a fortress of controlled chaos. Unframed canvases leaned against the walls in deep, dusty layers. Jars of murky water held brushes in a state of permanent soak. The floor was a treacherous landscape of tangled guitar cables and effects pedals, coiling like black, metallic vines around the legs of her easel. Outside her grimy, barred window, Mumbai was a restless sleeper, its low, constant hum a breath that promised to turn into a roar at any moment. It had broken many. It had not, yet, broken her.

The turpentine smell was particularly strong tonight, and it snagged on a memory, pulling her back to the clean, sharp scent of pine needles in the hills of Arunachal Pradesh. A place where the stars were so bright you could see the texture of the moon, and a smile was just a smile, not the prelude to a transaction. *"Mumbai eats girls like you, Chung,"* the voice of her grandmother echoed in her mind, a sad, old prophecy. She had come here to prove that voice wrong. Now, she just focused on not letting it have the last word.

That was why she had skipped the band jam with DeadLoo tonight. Her head was throbbing with a familiar, soul-deep exhaustion. She wasn't friends with her bandmates. She wasn't friends with anyone. Friendship was a currency of trust she couldn't afford to spend in a city where every handshake felt like an assessment and every casual touch felt like a trap. It was simply safer here, alone, with her paints and her guitar, building a wall around herself one forgery at a time.

She was adding a final dab of white to a water lily when a soft knock sounded at her door. It wasn't the usual impatient rap from her neighbor. This was quiet and hesitant, and it sent a sliver of ice down her spine. Her brush froze mid-air. Another knock, just as soft, was followed by a silence so complete it felt like a held breath. Heart hammering, she crept to the door and pressed her eye to the peephole. The hallway was empty. A cold knot of dread tightened in her gut. She double-checked the deadbolt, then moved through her small apartment, a silent shadow securing the window latches. It was as her hand touched the plug of her guitar amp that a low, rasping voice spoke from directly behind her, a violation so profound it felt like a physical blow.

"I knew you lived alone."

A choked, strangled gasp escaped her as she spun around. A man was standing in the middle of her living room. Her living room. He was just a dark shape against the window, but she could see the calm, predatory smile on his face and the hunger in his eyes.

"I've been following you, Chung," he said, taking a slow, deliberate step forward. Her mouth turned to sand.

"Get out of my house," she managed, her voice a dry rasp.

His smile widened, becoming a wolfish leer. "You act so tough on the street, playing that guitar. But I've watched you." As he spoke, her fear began to crystallize into a cold, sharp-edged focus. Her mind became a catalog of weapons: the heavy easel, the jars of turpentine, and the glass flower vase on the table behind her. Her hand began to move, slow and stealthy, behind her back.

He took another step, closing the distance. "You think you're special, but you're just another—"

She didn't let him finish. With a raw scream of fury, she grabbed the vase and hurled it. It flew through the air in a perfect, desperate arc and struck his forehead with a sickening, wet crack. He staggered back, his own scream a mixture of shock and pain as blood bloomed instantly from a deep gash over his eye.

"Bitch!" he hissed and lunged, no longer a calm predator but a wounded, raging animal.

She dodged, grabbing a dull palette knife from her worktable and slashing wildly. He ducked under her arm, his hand clamping onto her wrist with brutal strength. He twisted. A grinding, white-hot fire shot up her arm, a pain so intense it felt as if the bone itself was about to snap. A scream was ripped from her throat. He shoved her hard, but she planted her feet, using his own momentum against him. With every ounce of her survival instinct, every ounce of strength she had, she heaved her body forward into his. He was off-balance. He tripped backward over the low coffee table. The air was filled with a sickening percussion of shattering glass and a wet, final thud as his body crashed through it.

He lay sprawled in the wreckage, a broken marionette in a sea of glittering glass. Blood was pooling beneath him. For a long, panting second, Chung could only stare, the sound of her own heartbeat a thunderous roar in her ears. *Is he dead?* The question was a frantic whisper in a mind that was suddenly starved for air.

She stumbled backward, her limbs trembling uncontrollably, and burst onto the small balcony. She sucked in a lungful of damp night air, and her wet sock skidded on the slick, overwatered tiles. Her world pitched sideways in a violent, dizzying lurch. Her body was thrown forward, her torso tipping completely over the low, rusted railing. The city lights became a spinning, rushing abyss below her. For one horrifying, crystal-clear half-second, a single thought cut through her terror: *This is how it ends. Stupid. Pointless.* But instinct screamed louder. With a violent, animal contortion that sent a fresh agony through her injured arm, she twisted her body and slammed backward, crashing painfully into the rattan chair behind her.

She lay on the cold, wet tiles of the balcony, her breath coming in shallow, ragged gasps. Her mind felt strangely blank, muffled by a thick layer of shock. It was in this daze that she watched the sky above her burn. A silent, searing tear of impossible golden light ripped across the heavens. It was followed by a deep, bone-jarring roar that seemed to vibrate up from the center of the earth, a sound she felt more in her teeth than in her ears. For a long, stunned moment, she was pinned by the sensory assault, her mind wiped clean of thought. The bloody mess in her living room, the searing pain in her arm, the horrifying sensation of the fall—it all receded, dwarfed by the awesome, terrifying image of the universe screaming.

As the light faded and the sound died away, a profound silence descended, broken only by her own shuddering breaths. She sat up slowly, every muscle in her body a geography of new and old pains. The reality of her situation came crashing back, but it was now split in two. Behind her, through the open balcony door, was the first nightmare: a dead or dying man, blood on her floor, and a life sentence waiting for her. Ahead of her, on the distant horizon, was the second nightmare: a strange, violent fire, a wound in the city's fabric.

The first nightmare was an ending. The second was a question.

In that moment, a cold, clear survivor's logic cut through her panic. Her sanctuary was gone. Her life here was over. Survival meant moving, and the only direction that wasn't backward into a jail cell was forward, toward the fire. Without a second thought, she got to her feet, pulled on the first hoodie she could find, and shoved her blood-slick hands deep into the sleeves, hiding the evidence. She took one last look at her small apartment, no longer a home but a tomb for the life she had tried to build. Then she slipped out the door and into the night, a ghost leaving a ghost behind. Whatever had just fallen from the sky, it had given her a direction to run. And she was going to take it.

CHAPTER FOUR

DEV'S DESPERATION

The night air was a thick, foul cocktail of rotting garbage and diesel fumes that coated the back of his throat. Dev shifted the strap of his laptop bag again, the frayed canvas digging a raw furrow into his sore shoulder. His thin hoodie, soaked completely through, clung to his skin with a clammy, chilling weight, making every movement a small, miserable effort. A deep, grinding ache, born from too many hours standing at his low-paying job, radiated up from his legs. Two hours. A two-hour walk through the city's forgotten guts to a home that was little more than a place to sleep.

An auto would have cost fifty rupees. He saw one splash past him, its warm yellow light a fleeting temptation. But fifty rupees was a calculation he had made a thousand times. Fifty rupees was half a week of vegetables for Ma. It was another set of cheap glass bangles for Pihu's wedding. It was a choice between his own small comfort and their needs. It was never a choice at all. So he walked.

His thirty-thousand-rupee salary was a cruel joke, a brief visitor in his bank account. Twenty-eight thousand of it vanished in an automatic transfer the moment it arrived, a silent, digital offering for Pihu's wedding. Pihu, the stepsister who looked through him in public, whose smiling, perfect family photos posted online never, ever included his face. He was the ghost at her feast, the invisible benefactor of a life he wasn't invited to share. But the money wasn't for her, not really. It was for Ma, the woman who had taken him in after his own mother died, the woman who had fed him from her own plate and whose rough, kind hands had taught him everything he knew about enduring. Love, he told himself as filthy water seeped into his shoes, did not keep score.

The drizzle thickened into a steady, miserable rain, turning the potholed lanes into murky, ankle-deep streams. The numbness that had started in his toes was beginning to creep up his feet. The laptop on his back felt heavier than usual, its weight not just in the machine itself but in the crushing burden of the life it represented—the job he couldn't lose, the family he couldn't fail, the fragile scaffolding of a world he was barely holding together with his own two bleeding hands.

The angry, sputtering whine of two-stroke engines cut through the steady drumming of the rain. The sound was wrong, too close. Before he could react, two pairs of headlights sliced through the darkness, pinning him in their glare. Two motorcycles, carrying three shadowy figures, skidded to a halt in a wide, menacing semi-circle, their tires spraying muddy water. Their engines idled with a hungry, snarling growl. Instinct screamed at him to run, but his legs were frozen, his mind paralyzed by the sudden, predatory trap.

"Wallet, watch, phone," barked the man in the middle, brandishing a length of rusted iron rod.

The exhaustion in Dev's bones was so profound that there was no room for defiance. With trembling fingers, he pulled out his wallet, which held nothing but his ID. He unstrapped the fake Titan watch, the last gift from his mother. He handed over the cheap, taped-up phone. They were just things. He could endure their loss.

The man with the rod flipped through the empty wallet and sneered. "No money?"

Dev could only shake his head, his heart a frantic drum against his ribs.

The rod whistled through the wet air. The impact on his shoulder was a blinding flash of white-hot fire, a shockwave of pure agony that sent him stumbling sideways, a strangled gasp tearing from his throat.

"Where's the cash?" another one snarled, his voice a guttural growl.

"I don't have any," Dev choked out, clutching his shoulder, the pain so intense it made his vision swim.

Another blow, this one a solid, sickening thud against his ribs. The air was driven from his lungs in a pained, desperate whoosh, and the world dissolved into a tilting, nauseating blur. In that moment of disorientation, he felt a hand grab the strap of his laptop bag.

"No!" The word was a raw, primal croak, torn from a place deeper than pain. A switch flipped. The laptop. The job. The money for Pihu's wedding. The promise to Ma. Losing the bag wasn't a robbery; it was the complete annihilation of his entire world. Without a thought, he yanked the bag back, clutching it to his chest like a drowning man holding on to a piece of driftwood.

"Leave it, asshole!" one of them yelled, wrenching at the strap.

A surge of pure, desperate adrenaline coursed through him. He fought back, swinging the heavy bag like a club, fueled by a rage born of utter helplessness. He caught one of them in the chest, the impact sending the man staggering back in surprise. It was the opening he needed. He turned to run, his heart thundering. But his next step found only empty air. His foot plunged into the black, watery void of an open manhole he hadn't seen in the darkness. A sickening twist, a sharp, grinding spike of excruciating pain shot up his entire leg. A scream was ripped from his throat as he went down, his body crumpling onto the filthy pavement. The bag was torn from his grasp. The last thing he heard before the pain consumed him was the triumphant howl of their engines as they disappeared into the night, their taillights shrinking like cruel, red eyes.

Dev lay in the spreading puddle of filth and rain, the fight finally and completely gone from him. The rain hammered down, plastering his thin hoodie to his skin, washing the blood from his cheek into the cracks of the pavement. He tried to shift his weight, and a fresh, nauseating wave of agony from his ankle and ribs forced a pained gasp from his lips. With a final, grim effort, he dragged himself sideways, the rough asphalt tearing the skin from his palms, until he was out of the middle of the road. He rolled onto his back, the shocking cold of the concrete seeping through his wet clothes and into his bones. Tears of pure, impotent frustration finally came, hot against his cold skin. He hadn't just lost a laptop. He had failed. After a lifetime of simply enduring, he had failed at the one thing he was supposed to be good at.

"What now?" he whispered to the polluted, starless sky, the words a final, empty exhalation of surrender.

And the universe answered with violence.

A silent, blinding fissure of light tore the heavens open. It was not a gentle dawn; it was a brutal, instantaneous day, so brilliant it turned the grimy, rain-soaked world into a landscape of stark, painful white and razor-sharp black. For a single, suspended heartbeat, Dev's own pain was forgotten, his mind wiped clean by the sheer impossibility of the sight. A searing trail of fire punched through the clouds, a beautiful and terrifying scar carved across the sky.

The blast wave hit a moment later. It was not a sound he heard but a physical blow he felt. A deep, concussive boom that slammed up from the ground, vibrating through the pavement and into his aching ribs, making his teeth rattle in his skull. He cried out, instinctively curling into a ball as dust and bits of rust rained down from a nearby awning.

When the shuddering stopped, he lifted his head, blinking grit and rain from his eyes. Far in the distance, beyond the skeletal ruins of the old factories, a thick pillar of smoke was rising. And at its base, an orange glow pulsed with the steady, rhythmic beat of a new and monstrous heart. A beacon. The pain in his ankle was still a searing fire, but a new, more powerful force was pulling at him now. A primal, urgent need to move toward that light. He used a low wall to pull himself upright, a raw grunt of pain tearing from his throat. Cradling his bruised ribs, he took one agonizing, limping step, and then another, toward the impossible fire.

A low, guttural rumble rippled through the earth, a vibration that felt older and angrier than thunder. On the half-lit road, Rahul stumbled as the asphalt shivered beneath his feet. On the rooftop, Sujata felt the building tremble like a living thing. On her balcony, Chung gasped as her windows hummed with an unseen energy. And on the street, Dev felt the city itself growl in warning.

Then the sky cracked, and the shockwave rolled outward like a physical blow. Metal shutters clanged violently down narrow lanes. Car alarms began to shriek, one after another, in a rising chorus of mechanical panic. The city's stray dogs, silenced moments before, erupted in a unified, terrified howl. From the slums near the city's edge, human voices joined the chaos—shouts, prayers, and curses blending into a single sound of fear. Rumors ignited like sparks in dry grass: a bomb, a missile, the end of the world. Panic, raw and contagious, spilled into the streets as families poured from their homes, pointing toward the strange orange glow now pulsing against the horizon.

In the midst of the chaos, four souls moved with a singular, unspoken purpose. Rahul's heart pounded, and his feet, driven by an instinct older than reason, carried him toward the light. Sujata, her mind wiped clean of everything but the image of the burning sky, ran down the crumbling stairwell. Chung, breathless, stumbled out into the rain-slick street, her gaze locked on the distant fire. And Dev, gritting his teeth against the searing pain in his leg, dragged himself forward, pulled by a force stronger than his own agony.

They did not know each other. They did not know what they were running toward. But deep in the city's bones, an unspoken truth settled: whatever had fallen was not for the rich or the powerful. It was a dark miracle, sent for the desperate. It was for them. And if they were fast enough, they could claim it before the world even knew it was gone.

CHAPTER FIVE

STRANGERS IN THE SMOKE

The smoke coiled into the bruised night sky, a thick, greasy question mark asking a question the world didn't have an answer for. Even from the road, Rahul felt the heat—not the familiar, damp warmth of a Mumbai night, but a dry, baking heat that felt like standing too close to a kiln. He brought his Honda Shine to a sputtering halt, the engine giving one final, rattling cough before dying. The silence that rushed in was absolute, save for a high-pitched, electronic hum that seemed to vibrate in the fillings of his teeth.

He slid off the seat, his movements slow and clumsy, his limbs feeling heavy and disconnected from his brain. He pulled off his helmet, and the air that hit his face was a shock. It was thick with the acrid smell of scorched earth and superheated metal, but woven through it was something else, something utterly alien: a sweet, sharp scent like burning sugar and electricity that coated the back of his throat and made each breath feel like a strange, chemical intrusion.

A cold sweat plastered his cheap office shirt to his back, a chilling reminder of the man he had been just minutes before, the man who had been hurtling toward a concrete barrier. He looked at his own hands, the knuckles scraped raw and white from his death grip on the handlebars. He was still here. Alive. Breathing this strange, poisoned air. Every sane instinct screamed at him to turn around, to get back on the bike and ride as far and as fast as he could. But his feet felt leaden, rooted to the cracked, trembling ground.

He took one hesitant step forward. His worn-out shoe crunched on something that glittered. He looked down. The ground, the dead weeds, the scattered debris—everything was coated in a fine, shimmering dust that seemed to drink the moonlight and glow with a soft, internal luminescence. It was terrifying. It was beautiful. He took another step, then another, drawn forward by a force more powerful than his own fear. Ahead of him, the crater was a black, gaping mouth in the earth, steam curling from its edges in slow, ghostly tendrils. It felt alive, a sleeping, monstrous thing that had just fallen from the sky, and it was pulling him in.

The heat hit her like a physical wall. It was a dry, baking warmth that radiated from the ground, a stark and shocking contrast to the cold, whipping wind she had just left on the rooftop. Barefoot, she picked her way forward, each step a small, sharp agony. The ground was a treacherous carpet of broken debris, sharp gravel, and a strange, glittering dust that bit into the soft, tender soles of her feet. Her torn dress felt absurd, a cheap, flimsy costume from a life that had ended just an hour ago on that ledge.

Every survival instinct she had ever learned, every lesson the city had beaten into her, screamed at her to turn back, to disappear into the familiar, anonymous shadows. But the raw, pulsing energy from the crater was a strange and powerful magnet. Just moments ago, she had been ready to fall into nothing. Now, this impossible, burning hole in the earth offered something else. Not hope, but a question. A reason to take one more step.

Then she saw the silhouette. A man, standing near the crater's edge. Her blood ran cold. Her heart, which had been pounding with a wild awe, seized with a much older and more familiar fear. Her mind, conditioned by the predatory gazes of men like Vikrant, instantly screamed *danger*. She froze, her entire body a coiled spring, ready to bolt back into the darkness. But a wave of profound, bone-deep exhaustion washed over her, heavier than her fear. She was just so tired of running.

So she watched him. She forced her panicked breathing to slow, and she watched. He wasn't moving with purpose. He wasn't scanning the area for prey. His shoulders were slumped in a posture of utter defeat. He held his helmet not like a weapon, but like a heavy, useless burden. As her eyes adjusted to the strange, shimmering light, she saw it clearly. It was the posture of a man who had just lost a fight, a fight she knew in her own bones. He wasn't a hunter. He was another piece of wreckage, washed up on the shore of the same impossible disaster. He wasn't a threat. He was a mirror.

Chung approached from the east, a ghost moving through a field of ghosts. She used the twisted skeletons of dead trees and hulking piles of industrial debris for cover, her movements a fluid, practiced silence. The cold, wet sensation of blood soaking through her left sneaker was a constant, sharp reminder of the reason she could never go home again, a fact that had honed her senses to a razor's edge. Her hoodie was pulled low, her face a mask of shadow, and her hands clenched into tight, white-knuckled fists inside her pockets.

Her artist's eye, a tool she now used for survival, deconstructed the scene with a strange, cold detachment. The light emanating from the crater was all wrong—it was a painter's nightmare, casting shadows that were too long, too sharp, and seemed to writhe with a life of their own. She crouched behind a rusted metal drum and looked at the ground. It was coated in a fine, glittering powder that wasn't just reflecting the moonlight; it seemed to be generating its own faint, internal luminescence. She risked reaching out, rubbing a pinch between her fingers. It was gritty, surprisingly heavy, and felt strangely cool to the touch despite the heat radiating from the crater. It was not of this earth.

Her gaze shifted to the other figures. She cataloged them instantly. A middle-aged man in a cheap shirt, his body slumped in a posture of utter defeat. A woman in a torn party dress, barefoot, her stance a portrait of raw, bone-deep exhaustion. Chung's entire body tensed, every muscle coiling, ready to launch her back into the darkness. Her entire life in this city had been a series of carefully planned exits, and her instincts, honed by betrayal and violence, screamed that these strangers were an unknown variable she could not afford.

And yet, she did not run. It wasn't a mystical pull; it was a cold, hard calculation. She watched them for a full, silent minute, her breath held tight in her chest. They didn't speak. They didn't move toward each other. They simply stood in their separate worlds of pain, staring at the impossible hole in the ground. They weren't hunters. Their body language screamed victim. They were shipwrecked, just like her. The choice was simple: the certain danger of the body in her apartment or the potential danger of these two broken strangers. In a city that had just tried to kill her, this felt like the safest bet she could make.

Dev was the last to arrive, and his approach was a slow, agonizing pilgrimage of pain. He dragged his right leg through the mud, each step a fresh, grinding torment in his twisted ankle. With every shallow breath, his bruised ribs sent a sharp, stabbing protest through his side. The cold mud squelched in his single remaining shoe. Yet, he barely registered these sensations. His entire world, which just moments ago had shrunk to the size of a filthy puddle, had now expanded to a single, impossible focal point: the pulsing, orange glow ahead. It was a fierce and undeniable command, pulling him forward.

Then he saw them. Three dark figures, silhouetted against the hazy light of the crater. A jolt of pure, animal terror, a violent echo of the men in the alley, shot through him. *Danger.* His mind, still reeling from the attack, flooded with paranoia. Were there more of them? More scavengers drawn by the same light, waiting to pick off the next victim? He pictured another fight, another beating, and the final, humiliating loss. His body, already screaming in protest, threatened to give out, to simply collapse in the mud.

But something else rose up to meet the fear. A raw, ragged defiance. They had taken his wallet, his phone, his dignity. They had left him for dead. There was nothing more they could take from him. With a force of will that sent a fresh wave of agony through his body, he straightened his spine. He wiped the mixture of rain and blood from his brow with the back of a scraped hand and fixed his gaze on the three strangers. He would not hide. He would not run. He walked forward, deliberately putting weight on his injured leg, a silent, painful declaration: *See me. See that I am broken, but see that I am still here.*

They stood now, the four of them, a tense, unspoken circle around the crater's edge. The silence between them was thick and charged, buzzing with the leftover energy of the impact and the colliding waves of their individual traumas. They were four corners of a new, unstable world, each one a survivor, each one a potential enemy, and each one too fundamentally broken to do anything but stand their ground.

Rahul knew he had to be the one to speak. The silence was becoming its own kind of monster, thick with suspicion and the hum of the strange, hot earth. He cleared his throat, and the sound was a rough, ugly tear in the quiet.

"You... you saw it too?" he asked, the words shredded and hoarse. It wasn't just a question. It was a plea for sanity, a desperate hope that he hadn't finally, completely broken from reality. His gaze flickered uncertainly from the barefoot woman to the hooded girl and finally to the injured young man.

The woman in the torn dress gave a single, almost imperceptible nod, her arms still wrapped around herself as if holding her own pieces together. The woman in the hoodie offered only a stiff, defensive shrug, a gesture that admitted nothing. It was the young man who answered, a grim, broken smile briefly touching his lips.

"Yeah," he rasped, the word costing him a visible effort. "Hard to miss." He was immediately seized by a deep, wet cough that shook his entire body, and he winced, his hand flying to his bruised ribs.

Sujata's attention snapped into focus. In the strange, pulsing light from the crater, she could see the dark, damp smear of blood on his hoodie and the raw, angry scrape on his cheek. It was a kind of damage she recognized. It was the city's signature. Before her own fear could stop her, she was moving, a small, automatic act of care in a night that had been utterly savage. She fumbled in her battered purse, her fingers closing around a crumpled, forgotten tissue.

"You're bleeding," she said, her voice quiet as she stepped closer, holding it out.

Dev flinched. It was a full-body recoil, an instinct born from a life where every offered hand came with a hidden price. He stared at the small, white tissue as if it were a weapon. *What does she want?* His mind screamed. But when he looked up at her face, he saw no calculation in her eyes. He saw only a reflection of his own profound, bone-deep exhaustion. Slowly, his hand still shaking, he reached out and took it. His scraped, dirty fingers brushed against the tips of hers.

It wasn't a jolt. It was a shock of simple, human warmth against his cold skin, a sensation so foreign and unexpected it almost made him pull back. He just managed a short, stiff nod of thanks.

As this fragile truce was being forged, Rahul's attention was pulled back to the crater. He edged closer, his eyes fixed on a strange, liquid gleam in the scorched earth. It wasn't a reflection. It was a light that seemed to be coming from within the soil itself. Chung, her own curiosity overriding her caution, crouched beside him. With the careful precision of an artist, she reached out and brushed her fingers against a single, glittering particle. It was heavier than it looked. She picked it up, holding it aloft in the moonlight. It wasn't just a rock. It pulsed with a soft, internal light, a tiny, captive star.

"Gold," she whispered.

The word, spoken with a reverence that was completely alien to her, hung in the air like a second, smaller explosion.

Sujata gasped, her hand flying to her mouth. Dev, his pain and his paranoia momentarily forgotten, stared with wide, disbelieving eyes.

"You're kidding," Rahul muttered, but a wild, terrifying hope was already pounding in his chest. He didn't just kneel; he dropped, plunging his hands into the warm, strange soil with a desperate, almost feral need to know. He scooped up a clump of earth. It was heavy in his palms. He let it crumble through his fingers, and there, nestled in the black dirt, were dozens of tiny, gleaming, unmistakably metallic pellets. He rose to his feet slowly, as if in a dream, and turned to the others, his hand outstretched and trembling.

"This," he said, his voice shaking with the sheer, impossible weight of the miracle in his palm, "this is real."

A profound, stunned silence descended, deeper and more complete than before. The only sound was the soft, steady hiss of the cooling crater. The city, with all its noise and cruelty and demands, felt a million miles away. Here, in this impossible moment, four strangers stood on the precipice of a new world, with no idea if it had come to save them or to damn them completely.

CHAPTER SIX

ASHES AND INTRODUCTIONS

They fell upon the crater's edge like starving animals. The earth was a strange, alien substance—not soft mud, but a thick, greasy paste fused with sharp, glassy fragments that tore at their fingertips. Beneath the surface, the ground was a brittle, layered crust, a bizarre geology of baked earth and molten rock that fought their every effort.

Rahul, fueled by a lifetime of pent-up frustration, wielded a broken iron rod like a weapon. He slammed it into the stubborn ground, each impact a jarring shock that vibrated up his soft, office-worker arms. The pain was immediate, but it was a clean pain, a productive pain, a welcome antidote to the years of quiet, soul-crushing humiliation. Sweat poured down his face, mixing with the grime, as he worked with a grunt and a curse, exorcising his old self with every blow.

Dev was a study in pure, agonizing willpower. Every time he shifted his weight onto his injured ankle, a wave of white-hot fire shot up his leg. Every scoop he made with a jagged piece of rusted sheet metal sent a sharp, stabbing protest from his bruised ribs. He moved with a stiff, jerky rhythm, his face a tight mask of concentration. The only thing that kept him from screaming was the sight of the gold, a hypnotic, glittering promise in the dirt that was a more potent painkiller than any drug.

Sujata, kneeling, had abandoned all caution. The moment her dress snagged and tore with a sharp rip, a switch flipped in her mind. The fear of a ruined dress, of dirty hands, of a broken nail—these were luxuries for a life she no longer lived. She dug with her bare hands, a frantic, desperate energy driving her as she clawed at the strange soil. Her palms were quickly scraped raw, the thin lines of blood that welled up instantly swallowed by the black, glittering mud. The pain was a distant, unimportant fact. The only thing that was real was the image of Anaya's face, a face she would save with this dirt, this blood, this pain.

Chung worked with a chilling, methodical efficiency. While the others waged a brute-force war on the ground, she moved with the precision of an artist, her eyes seeing the patterns of the impact, her fingers tracing the most promising veins of material. Her delicate hands, usually deft with a paintbrush, were now caked in a thick, bloody paste, but they moved with a tireless, focused energy. With every scoop, she was not just digging for gold; she was digging away from the memory of the body in her apartment, trying to outrun the ghost that was waiting for her back home. The only sounds in the universe were the scrape of metal on stone, their own ragged breaths, and the soft, menacing hiss of the earth as it cooled around them. They worked under a vast, pitiless sky, four desperate souls digging for their lives.

After what felt like an eternity of frantic, silent labor, Rahul had to stop. Panting, his lungs burning, he stabbed the iron rod into the earth and leaned his full weight on it, his whole body trembling with exhaustion. He looked at the three strangers working alongside him, their faces grim masks of mud and sweat, all of them moving with the same desperate, consuming fire. The question had been a burning ember in his mind.

"You all live... around here?" he asked, his voice a rough, dust-coated rasp.

Sujata didn't pause in her work, her fingers skillfully prying a small, gleaming nugget from a chunk of fused earth. She brushed a muddy strand of hair from her forehead with the back of her wrist. "Kamraj Nagar," she answered, the name of the sprawling, forgotten slum, a simple, tired statement of fact.

Chung, still crouched low to the ground like a predator over its kill, merely jerked her chin to the west without looking up. "Behind the old bus depot," she said, her tone clipped and final, a clear boundary line drawn in the dirt. *That is all you get from me.*

Dev paused, the effort of his makeshift shovel making him wince. He wiped a smear of mud from his cheek with a grimy sleeve. "A chawl, next to the dump yard," he muttered, the words an apology.

"It's a fifteen-minute walk if the lanes aren't flooded and the rats stay out of your way."

A short, breathless, and utterly bitter chuckle escaped Rahul's lips. "Figures."

"Figures what?" Dev asked, his voice instantly sharp with suspicion, his hands freezing over a patch of glittering soil.

Rahul gave a weary shrug, a motion that sent a fresh ache through his overtaxed shoulders. He looked from one battered, mud-streaked face to the next, and in their exhausted, haunted eyes, he saw a perfect, soul-crushing reflection of his own desperation.

"Only the broken ones," he said, his voice quiet but carrying with a strange clarity over the hiss of the crater, "would be out chasing falling stars at midnight."

The words landed with the force of a physical blow. For the first time, Sujata stopped digging. Her hands, raw and bleeding, fell to her lap. She looked up at him, and a small, sad smile of pure, aching recognition touched her lips. It was a smile completely devoid of humor, a silent acknowledgment that said, *You see me. You finally, truly see me.*

A moment later, Chung let out a short, sharp snort from under her hood. It was not a sound of amusement. It was the sound of a bitter, surprising agreement, the sound a lone wolf might make upon discovering it is not, in fact, the only one of its kind in the forest.

Dev's rusted piece of sheet metal struck something solid with a dull, heavy thud. He grunted, digging around it, and pried a large, fist-sized clump of fused earth and rock from the ground. As he turned it over in his hands, the dirt crumbled away under his thumbs, revealing a dense network of gleaming, molten metal threaded through the rock, so bright it seemed to pulse with its own internal light. He let out a low, breathless whistle that cut through the night.

"This..." he said, his voice a hoarse, reverent whisper, a sound of dawning, terrifying wonder. "This has to be worth lakhs. Maybe crores."

The word *"crores"* hung in the air, a sound so impossibly large it seemed to change the very atmosphere. Sujata and Rahul scrambled closer, their own fatigue forgotten, their eyes wide with a shared, greedy awe. But Chung was already moving. She knelt beside Dev and, without asking, took the heavy clump from his hands. Her touch was not gentle; it was the practical, analytical grip of an appraiser. She scraped at the surface with a dirty fingernail and weighed it in her palm, her expression hardening into a grim mask.

"Maybe," she said, her voice a sharp, cold anchor in their sudden sea of euphoria. "It's worth it if we don't get arrested. It's worth it if we don't get murdered for it. And it's worth that," she paused, her gaze moving from one stunned face to the next, a slow, deliberate, and deeply suspicious scan, "if one of us doesn't decide to take it all and screw the other three over."

Her words fell into the silence like chunks of ice, instantly extinguishing the warm, fragile flame of their hope. The unspoken dangers—the police, the city's predators, and now, each other—were suddenly named, ugly, and real. The fragile "we" that had been forming between them shattered. In that heavy, poisoned silence, the dream of Anaya's surgery, the vision of a life free from Meghna, the simple hope of an escape from poverty—all of it suddenly felt terrifyingly vulnerable. For the first time, they realized their greatest threat might not be the world outside but the person standing right next to them in the dark.

Sujata looked at the circle of suspicious faces and knew she had to break it. "I don't care about getting rich," she said, her voice soft but carrying a surprising firmness that cut through the tension. "I just need enough."

The words were so unexpected they made everyone pause their digging. Rahul looked over, his hard expression softening with a flicker of curiosity. "Enough for what?" he asked, his tone gentler than he intended.

Sujata took a deep breath; the decision to share her deepest wound was a terrifying gamble. But it was the only truth she had. "My niece," she said, her voice cracking slightly. "She's sick. Very sick. She needs surgeries I can't afford. I lost my sister last year, and I promised her... I promised I would take care of her little girl." The words hung in the air, heavy and irrefutable. Dev glanced at her, then quickly looked away, a silent gesture of respect for a grief too raw to be stared at. Rahul gave a slow, solemn nod. Promises made to the dying were a language he understood.

Sujata wiped her muddy hands on her torn dress, her gaze finding Rahul's. "So what about you? What hole are you trying to climb out of?"

A harsh, barking laugh, completely devoid of humor, escaped Rahul's lips. "A boss who thinks my job description includes being her personal plaything," he said, the bitterness scorching every word. "And a life that reminds me every single day that I'm too old, too poor, and too replaceable to matter."

No one offered a single, empty word of sympathy. They just absorbed the raw, ugly truth of it.

Dev cleared his throat, wincing as the movement pulled at his bruised ribs. "My stepsister's wedding," he muttered, his eyes fixed on the ground. "Every rupee I earn is for her. The reason I got my ass kicked tonight," he gestured to his bruised face, "was trying to save the office laptop I need to keep sending that money." He let out a broken, self-deprecating chuckle. "Didn't even save it."

"You tried," Sujata said, her voice a soft anchor in his sea of failure. Dev looked up at her, and in their long, shared gaze, a silent understanding passed between them.

Before the moment could settle, Chung's voice sliced through the air, utterly flat and devoid of emotion.

"My stalker is probably dead in my living room."

The statement landed with the force of a physical explosion, shattering the night. They all turned to stare at her, their own problems instantly vaporized by the sheer horror of her words. She didn't flinch, but her hands, which had been sifting methodically through the dirt, were now moving with a frantic, violent energy, as if she could claw a hole in the earth and bury her own confession. Dev swallowed hard, his throat suddenly tight. Rahul opened his mouth, then shut it again, utterly lost.

It was Sujata who moved. Pushed by a profound, primal instinct of shared trauma, she reached out and rested her dirty, scraped hand on Chung's trembling shoulder. Chung's entire body went rigid, a violent, full-body flinch away from the unexpected touch. But she didn't pull away. For a long, agonizing moment, she remained frozen. Then, the rigid line of her shoulder softened, just a fraction, a near-imperceptible surrender to the small, fragile gesture of trust. In that moment, they looked at each other, four broken pieces of a city that had tried to throw them away. They had found something impossible. Something dangerous. And now, something irrevocably shared. A silent agreement passed between them. A silent beginning.

CHAPTER SEVEN

Morning After Myths

The sun rose over Mumbai not with a triumphant golden blaze, but like a slow, grudging apology. Its light, a weak and hazy orange, filtered through the city's perpetual smog, doing little to warm the profound chill that had settled deep in their bones. Inside the hollow shell of the abandoned warehouse, the morning felt like a dream. A single, sharp beam of light speared through a hole in the rusted ceiling, a theatrical spotlight that illuminated a lazy, mesmerizing swirl of dust motes and landed squarely on the strange, pathetic altar at the center of their new world.

Their treasure was not a gleaming chest of pirate fantasy. It was a messy, humble pile of small, uneven bundles wrapped in dirty cloth and tied with frayed rope, looking more like lumps of garbage than the keys to a new life. The feverish, frantic energy of the night's digging had completely evaporated, leaving behind a profound, bone-deep exhaustion and the sharp, metallic tang of fear in the air.

Rahul rubbed at his stiff shoulders, a pained wince twisting his face as his joints cracked in loud protest. Every muscle in his body, soft from years behind a desk, screamed from the unaccustomed labor. But it was a good pain, a real pain, and he found he preferred it to the numb ache of his old life. Hope, he was discovering, was a much heavier burden than despair.

Sujata stifled a yawn, her eyes swollen and raw. The adrenaline that had propelled her through the night had vanished, leaving a hollow, buzzing fatigue that made the world feel distant and muffled. She stared at the cloth bundles, and the image of Anaya's face—her small, trusting smile—flashed in her mind with an almost painful intensity. For the first time in a year, the future was not a solid black wall but a terrifying, blindingly bright light she was afraid to look at directly.

Dev sat slumped against a concrete pillar, his bruised knuckles a stark contrast to the pale, determined set of his face. He swore under his breath as his cracked phone failed, yet again, to find a signal. An obsessive need gnawed at him: he had to see the news. He had to know if the world had even noticed that the sky had fallen. Every failed attempt felt like a confirmation that they were utterly, terrifyingly alone in this, adrift on an ocean of a secret too vast to comprehend.

A few feet away, Chung was a statue of coiled stillness, her knees drawn up to her chest. With a small, sharp twig, she methodically sketched intricate spirals and craters in the thick dust on the floor, the only thing in the universe she could control. Chung stopped sketching and looked at the nearest bundle. "We need to be careful with how we handle this stuff," she said, her voice dropping to a low, cautious murmur.

Rahul frowned, pausing his massage of his aching shoulders. "What do you mean? It's gold, Chung. It's a miracle."

"It's a rock that just cooked itself at 3,000 degrees in the atmosphere," she countered, pointing a twig at the glittering dust. "I've worked with heavy metal pigments in the studio—cobalt, lead, and cadmium. They're toxic if you breathe them in. This stuff has a smell like... like ozone and burnt sugar. We don't know what else is mixed in there besides the gold. If we're going to melt it, we do it in a ventilated space. No one breathes the fumes. We use gloves, or we wrap our hands."

Dev looked at his raw, scraped knuckles, a new flicker of worry in his eyes. "You think it's radioactive?"

"I think it's alien," Chung said simply. "And in this city, anything that looks like a gift usually comes with a slow-acting poison. We treat it like it's loaded, even when we're selling it."

No one spoke. No one dared to suggest they leave. The gold was the chain that held them here, but their shared, unspeakable trauma was the lock. They were bound by the certain knowledge that no one else on earth would ever understand what had happened in the darkness and by the terrifying, fragile hope that it might have just saved them all.

"Alright," Rahul said, his voice a rough rasp that scraped against the heavy silence. He dragged a hand through his disheveled hair, the gesture doing nothing to calm the frantic, high-pitched hum of anxiety under his skin. "We need a plan. A real one. Now."

Dev looked up from his useless phone, his expression grim. "One thing's for sure," he said, his voice low and certain. "We can't just walk into Zaveri Bazaar with this. That place is a closed world. Generations of families. They'll smell us coming a mile away. We'd either get robbed in a back alley or they'd make one quiet phone call, and we'd be in a police station before we could even ask for a price."

The finality in his tone was crushing. Sujata frowned, a worried line creasing her brow as she ran a dirt-smudged thumb along the frayed edge of one of the bundles. "But... can't we just melt it down ourselves? Somewhere? Sell it as simple scrap gold?"

Chung, who had been watching them all with a detached, unnerving calm, let out a short, sharp laugh devoid of all humor. "Sure," she said, her voice dripping with a brutal sarcasm that made Sujata flinch. "And where do we plan on doing that? In your kitchen? With a blowtorch? Four broke nobodies, reeking of desperation, showing up at a scrap dealer with kilos of unrefined, unmarked, and probably radioactive space metal is the kind of story that doesn't have a happy ending. It ends with our pictures in the newspaper and our bodies in a morgue."

A heavier, more profound silence fell, the weight of Chung's words crushing the fragile hope that had begun to bloom in the morning light. Reality, cold and sharp, bit into them. They possessed a treasure they couldn't spend, a miracle they couldn't claim.

"Wait," Dev muttered, a new urgency in his voice. He pulled a frayed charger cord from his pocket, the wire held together with strips of black duct tape. He found a battered socket panel on a nearby pillar and jammed the plug in, wiggling it like a safecracker until a tiny red light flickered to life on his phone. "Give me a second," he said, his eyes scanning the rusted ceiling. "There has to be a loophole."

The other three watched, their breath held, as he angled the phone, hunting for a single, elusive bar of signal. The seconds stretched into minutes, each one filled with the distant, indifferent sounds of the waking city. Finally, a single, weak bar appeared. Dev's fingers flew across the cracked screen. His face was a mask of intense concentration.

"Found something," he said at last, his voice tight with a mixture of excitement and disbelief.

They instantly crowded around him, their shoulders touching, a small island of shared, desperate hope. On the screen was an article from an obscure science blog. Dev read the key sentences aloud, his voice gaining strength with each word.

"...traces of gold... rare, but not impossible... selling meteorite-derived metals is technically legal, *unless* the government officially claims the fall site first..." He paused, his eyes wide as he scanned the rest of the text. "Here it is. This is it. The loophole isn't about what it is; it's about what we *call* it. We don't call it meteorite gold. We melt it down ourselves, in small batches. Blend it with other cheap metals. And we sell it, piece by piece, as recycled scrap."

"It's doable," Dev breathed, a fragile, trembling thread of hope returning to his voice.

"If we are incredibly careful," Rahul added, his mind already racing with the logistics.

Sujata looked from one face to the next at the three exhausted, dirty, and dangerous strangers who now held her and Anaya's entire future in their hands. "It's only doable," she said quietly, her voice barely a whisper, "if we trust each other."

The words dropped into the dusty air like stones into a deep, silent well. The real problem was not the gold. It was them. Trust wasn't a luxury for people like them. It was everything.

Chung stood up abruptly, the sudden movement startling in the still air. She stretched until her spine cracked loudly, a sound of decision. "We split it now," she said, her voice sharp and practical, slicing through their haze of doubt. "And we hide it before the sun is fully up."

"How?" Sujata asked, her brow furrowed with confusion. "Where in this city can you hide something like this?"

A thin, sharp smile, the smile of a fox, touched Chung's lips. "You're thinking like someone who has something to lose," she explained, her voice a low, instructional murmur. "Rich people have safes and bank vaults. We have to think about what we are. We're invisible. We hide it in plain sight, in places no one with money would ever look twice. A loose brick in a chawl wall. The hollowed-out leg of a broken chair. The bottom of a garbage drum." She looked at their stunned, uncomprehending faces. "Nobody ever questions a poor person digging through trash. They expect it. Our poverty is our best camouflage."

Dev let out a soft, disbelieving chuckle that was thick with irony. "So we hide a fortune by pretending to be beggars."

Rahul clapped him on the shoulder, a cloud of dust rising from the impact. "Better a hidden beggar than a dead king," he said.

And for the first time, a sound that was not born of pain or fear passed between them. It started with Dev's chuckle, was met by Rahul's weary grin, and then blossomed into a rough, rusty, and utterly real laugh, shared by all four. It was the broken, beautiful sound of a tension so immense it had no choice but to finally shatter.

The laughter died down, leaving a new, fragile quiet in its wake. Without a word, they turned to the pile. This was the true test. There was no scale, no way to measure, no way to know if one share was greater than another. Any one of them could have started an argument that would have destroyed them. None of them did. In a slow, silent, and deeply profound act of blind faith, they simply divided the crude bundles into four roughly equal piles.

Sujata, her movements careful and reverent, wrapped her share in the tattered remains of her scarf. Dev, his hands surprisingly steady, tucked his bundle into a hidden inner pocket of his hoodie. Rahul, ever the pragmatist, found a discarded, grease-stained courier envelope in a pile of trash and slipped his portion inside. And Chung, with the practiced, secret ease of a smuggler, unzipped a false lining in her battered guitar case and hid her share within its padded walls.

When it was done, they stood facing each other. The air was different. They were four strangers, bound by a secret that could get them killed.

"We meet here tomorrow night," Rahul said, his voice taking on the natural authority of a leader.

"And we need a way to stay in touch," Dev added, holding up his battered, barely working phone. "What about a group chat?"

They all stared at him as if he'd just suggested forming a marching band.

"With fake names, obviously," he added sheepishly.

A long beat of silence, and then, a slow smile spread across Sujata's exhausted face. "Alright," she said. "Fake names it is."

Awkwardly, like teenagers who had just pulled off a magnificent prank, they swapped numbers. Rahul, with a weary sigh of acceptance at the new title he'd been given, became **Uncle Starfall**. Sujata, thinking of the red dress and the impossible moonlit night, chose **Scarlet Moon**. Chung, with a wry, self-deprecating smirk, typed in **Deadbeat Dreamer**. And Dev, grinning with a relief so profound it was almost painful, entered himself as **Wanderwolf**.

It was a stupid, reckless, and utterly perfect beginning. As they finally left the warehouse, scattering in four different directions like seeds on the wind, a single, unifying thought settled in each of them. The gold from the sky was the reason they had met, but it was their shared, broken humanity—and the fragile, foolish, and absolutely necessary trust they had just forged—that might actually be the thing that saved them.

CHAPTER EIGHT

WHISPERS IN THE DUST

By mid-morning, the heat had returned, not as a gentle warmth, but as an old, unwelcome guest settling its oppressive weight over the city. It was the thick, suffocating Mumbai heat that clung to the skin like a film of oil, that crawled into the lungs with every breath, and that seeped into the very bones until all energy was leached away. It was a heat that made the asphalt itself seem to sweat, that sent the stray dogs searching for slivers of shade, that drew a constant stream of quiet curses from the street vendors. And today, it carried with it the familiar city smells of hot tar, human sweat, and rotting fruit, but woven through them was something new: the invisible, electric scent of old secrets and new, terrifying lies.

The world spun on, a great, indifferent machine. The local trains were still packed with bodies, the traffic still snarled in a cacophony of horns, the great pretense of normalcy was in full, glorious effect. The city was pretending, as it always did, that nothing extraordinary had happened in the deep hours of the night. It was pretending that the sky had not cracked open, that a piece of it had not fallen to the earth, and that four broken lives had not just been torn apart and stitched back together into something new, fragile, and dangerous.

The ride back to his flat was a waking nightmare. Every pothole that jarred the bike's frame sent a fresh spike of terror through him, his mind instantly picturing the flimsy courier envelope tearing, spilling a river of impossible, glittering dust across the dirty Mumbai asphalt. A police van passed him, and his blood ran cold. He was sure they were slowing down, sure they were watching him. A group of men laughing on a street corner became a gang of thieves, their eyes following the bulge of his bag. The city, which had always ignored him, now felt alive with a million hostile eyes, all focused on the impossible secret he carried.

When he finally reached his building, the familiar shabbiness of his flat no longer felt like a prison; it felt like a trap. The flimsy lock on the door was a joke. The walls were thin enough to hear his neighbor's coughing. He looked at the single, grimy window that faced a concrete wall and saw not a barrier, but an entry point. He placed the bag on his thin mattress with the gingerly reverence of a man handling a live bomb. He peeled off his mud-caked clothes, his mind a frantic, racing engine of fear. He was free, he told himself, as long as he could remain a ghost.

He had been home for less than five minutes when a sharp, authoritative knock rattled the thin wooden door. Rahul froze, his heart leaping into his throat. *Police. They found me.* He crept to the door, his bare feet making no sound on the cool floor, and pressed his eye to the peephole. His terror was instantly replaced by a different, more familiar kind of dread. Mr. Chavan from next door. A retired government clerk whose life's sole remaining purpose seemed to be the relentless, forensic observation of his neighbors' lives.

"Rahul-ji?" Chavan's wheezy, penetrating voice called through the door. "Saw your light on. Back so early today? Everything alright?"

Rahul took a deep, steadying breath, trying to slow the frantic hammering of his heart. He pasted a mask of weary normalcy onto his face before cracking the door open just a few inches. "Yes, Chavan saab. Everything is fine. Just some early fieldwork. Vendor site inspections," he said, the lie feeling clumsy and obvious in his mouth.

Chavan's small, beady eyes ignored him completely, darting past his face to scan the room. Inevitably, they landed on the courier bag sitting on the bed. "Important vendor files, is it?" he asked, his voice thick with a casual, cloying skepticism that set Rahul's teeth on edge.

"Month-end pressure," Rahul replied, forcing a shrug, trying to keep his own voice from shaking. "You know how it is." A bead of sweat trickled down his spine. The silence that followed was a physical weight. He could feel his neighbor's suspicion, a tangible, suffocating force pressing in on him through the small crack in the door.

"Hmm," Chavan grunted finally, a single, noncommittal sound that was a full and complete judgment.

Desperate to end the ordeal, Rahul forced another weak smile. "I'll bring you some chai later, Uncle, once I settle in."

Chavan gave a slow, deliberate nod, his eyes making one final, lingering pass over the bag before he finally shuffled away. Rahul didn't move from the door until he heard the click of his neighbor's lock. Only then did he bolt his own door and lean his forehead against the cool, splintered wood, his entire body trembling with the aftershock of the encounter. Paranoia wasn't just a feeling anymore. It was a full-time job. It was the price of survival.

Sujata's journey home was a desperate navigation through a city of threats. She kept her head down, her path a frantic weave through the darkest shadows of the narrow lanes. The weight of the gold in her purse felt like a physical accusation, pulling her shoulder down. Every man who glanced at her as she passed became an informant for Vikrant, every police officer on a corner a secret agent from a government that had surely discovered its fallen star. By the time she reached her building, her hands were shaking so badly it took three attempts to get the key into the lock. The familiar groan of the door as she forced it open sounded like a scream in the quiet hallway.

The moment the bolt slid home, the familiar smell of her small world enveloped her: dust, the faint hint of mildew from the monsoon, and the lingering, sweet scent of Anaya's talcum powder. It was the smell of safety, of the one clean thing in her life. Her eyes immediately went to the crayon drawings taped to the wall—a lopsided sun, a flower with too many petals. These were the sacred texts of her life, the reason she had risked everything. She dropped her purse onto the sagging couch as if it were a venomous snake.

She knelt on the floor and, with trembling fingers, unwrapped the tattered scarf. In the dim, forgiving light of her apartment, the meteorite gold didn't look like salvation. It looked alien, a piece of a violent, predatory world she had just brought into her only sanctuary. Its unnatural gleam felt like a contamination. A wave of pure, suffocating terror washed over her. The thin walls of the flat suddenly felt like paper. She could hear Mrs. Joshi from upstairs yelling at her husband, her voice a sharp, percussive intrusion. How could she possibly keep a secret this large in a place built of no secrets at all? One curious question from a neighbor about a new dress for Anaya, one slip of the tongue at the market, and it would all be over. The gold would be gone. Anaya's future would be gone.

Her phone, which had slipped from her purse, buzzed sharply against the concrete floor. She flinched violently, her mind screaming a single name: *Vikrant*. For a heart-stopping second, she was frozen, expecting a threat, an ultimatum. But when she finally dared to look at the screen, it wasn't him. It was the group chat.

Wanderwolf: All good?

The simple question was a lifeline thrown into the churning waters of her panic. She watched as the other messages appeared, a cascade of shared, frantic paranoia that, paradoxically, made her feel instantly, incredibly calm.

Wanderwolf: Well... Nosey neighbors though.

Uncle Starfall: Ditto. I think Chavan uncle suspects I'm smuggling coconuts.

Deadbeat Dreamer: Chill. Trust no one. Act broke. Stay broke.

A sound that was half sob, half laugh escaped her lips, a startling, messy, and utterly genuine noise in the tense silence of the room. It was insane. It was reckless. But reading their words, she felt the crushing, isolating weight of her fear lift, just slightly. She was not alone in this terror. Her fingers still trembled as she typed her reply, but they trembled now with a newfound sense of resolve.

Scarlet Moon: Safe. You?

It wasn't just a message. It was a confirmation. They weren't just four strangers anymore. They were four points of a new, sharp, and dangerous constellation, navigating the same dark sky together.

Across town, Chung was waging a furious, silent war on her own apartment. On her hands and knees, she scrubbed the floorboards with a punishing, frantic energy, the harsh scrape of the brush against the cheap wood a counter-rhythm to the frantic drumming of her own heart. The air was thick with the suffocating, chemical smell of bleach, a sterile scent she was using to try and erase the memory of another, coppery one. This wasn't cleaning; it was an exorcism. Every speck of dust was an accusation, every lingering stain a phantom trace of the blood that had violated her sanctuary, a sanctuary she now realized had only ever been an illusion.

With every punishing pass of the brush, her mind snagged on the loose floorboard beneath her mattress. Underneath it, the guitar case, heavy with its impossible, glittering secret, felt less like an instrument and more like a live bomb, ticking silently in the heart of her newly sterile space. The contrast was a form of madness: a floor clean enough to eat off of and a secret dirty and dangerous enough to end her life. The very thing that promised freedom was also the thing that had her trapped in this room, scrubbing at ghosts.

The creak of a floorboard from the apartment above made her freeze, her body instantly rigid, the brush held motionless in her hand. *Boots.* Her mind screamed the word. But it was just the neighbor. A shout from the street below made her flinch, her head snapping toward the window. But it was just children playing. Every sound was a potential threat, every creak the prelude to the splintering of her door.

Finally, her muscles screaming in protest, she paused. She pushed herself to her feet and leaned against the cracked window, wiping a slick of sweat from her brow with the back of her arm. Below, a stray dog sniffed through a pile of garbage. A paanwala, in a cloud of his own lazy boredom, swatted at flies. The city, in its vast, grinding indifference, moved on, completely unaware of the dead man, the fallen star, or the storm that had already begun inside the walls of this small, silent room.

Dev, meanwhile, navigated a different kind of battlefield, one of familiar faces and prying eyes. He limped into the narrow, crowded lane of his chawl, the air thick with the smell of frying onions and damp laundry. He clutched a grocery bag stuffed with old newspapers, a prop designed to justify the unnatural weight of his share of the gold. He forced his face into a mask of utter exhaustion, a look so familiar on him that no one should question it. *Don't look up. Don't make eye contact. Just be the same tired boy you were yesterday.*

He passed Mrs. Pinto from 12B, who was standing at her doorway, her arms crossed, her suspicious glare a physical force that seemed to follow him down the lane. He gave her a small, tired nod, just as he always did, and kept moving. He passed the group of taxi drivers playing cards on an overturned crate, their loud, boisterous laughter a sound from a different, carefree universe. He was an actor on a high wire, and his only camouflage was to be exactly who he had always been: poor, tired, and utterly invisible.

He finally reached his door, his hand trembling as he fumbled for the key. He could feel Mrs. Pinto's eyes still on his back. He slipped into the small, dingy room and, without even turning on the light, bolted the door. The moment the heavy bolt slid home with a satisfying thud, the performance was over. The mask of normalcy dissolved, and a wave of tremors wracked his body. He pressed his forehead against the cool, peeling paint of the door, his legs shaking from the combined strain of his injury and the immense effort of acting normal. He had made it. He was still breathing. And for the first time, in the stifling, lonely quiet of his tiny room, he allowed himself to believe that he might actually have a dream worth protecting.

Later that night, as the city's roar finally softened to a distant hum, four small, cracked screens lit up in four separate, lonely rooms, a fragile web of connection in the vast, dark city.

Deadbeat Dreamer: Any heat?

Uncle Starfall: Neighbor questions. Nothing serious. I think.

Wanderwolf: Same here. Staying low.

Scarlet Moon: Me too. We need to be careful. What's the plan for tomorrow?

Deadbeat Dreamer: Melt a small batch. Test the waters. Find a quiet street jeweler who doesn't ask questions.

Wanderwolf: We do it together.

Scarlet Moon: Together.

The word, glowing on their separate screens, was a quiet, desperate promise. But beyond the fragile peace of their secret chat, the city's predators were stirring.

In a grimy, smoke-filled bar where the air was sour with spilled whiskey, Vikrant's rage had curdled into a cold, obsessive need for revenge. He pulled out his phone and scrolled to a contact saved as "Rats," a man who traded in the city's dirtiest secrets. The informant picked up on the first ring. "I'm looking for a girl," Vikrant snarled, his voice a low growl. "Works the bars. Her name is Sujata. Find her, and find out who she's with. I'll pay double your usual rate." He hung up, a cruel, satisfied smile twisting his lips.

Miles away, in a dimly lit shack that smelled of damp earth and cheap bidis, one of the thieves who had mugged Dev pressed a dirty cloth to the dark, angry bruise on his ribs. The memory of the boy's unexpected resistance was a source of deep, personal humiliation. "He fought like a cornered animal for that stupid bag," he growled to his companions. "An empty bag? No. There was something in it. I want to find that boy. I want to find out what he thought was worth taking a beating for. And then I want to take it from him."

And in a dusty, silent government office, under the weak glow of a single desk lamp, Inspector D'Souza laid out three separate files on his desk. The first was the seismic report, showing a significant, unclassified impact event. The second contained the brief, dismissed reports from two late-night airline pilots about an "unusual atmospheric flare." The third was a decades-old survey map. With a ruler and a pen, he drew two lines, triangulating the data. The lines intersected at one, precise location: the abandoned textile grounds. His brow furrowed. Unreported strikes were a bureaucratic mess. They were also, for a man with ambition, a rare opportunity. He opened his logbook and, with a neat, precise hand, wrote: *Investigate anomaly. Unofficial site visit required.* The city was waking up to their secret. The hunters were sharpening their knives. The four of them, finding a moment of comfort in their shared, digital space, had no idea the hunt had already begun.

CHAPTER NINE

THE PRICE OF SECRETS

They met as the sky over Mumbai bruised from a hazy grey to a deep, starless purple. The usual roar of the city seemed to recede into a low, distant growl, leaving the area around the abandoned warehouse in a pocket of tense, watchful silence. Inside, the air was cold and thick with a nervous energy so palpable it felt like static on the skin. Tonight, they carried something far heavier than gold. They carried intent.

Rahul arrived first, a ghost slipping through the deepening shadows. He moved with his head down, his eyes constantly scanning, every distant shout or backfiring engine a potential threat that sent a jolt of ice through his veins. He had deliberately shed the skin of Rahul Sharma, corporate failure. In a wrinkled cotton kurta and worn sandals, he was a tired, invisible man, a face the city was trained to overlook. The gold dust, secured in the double lining of his old satchel, was a heavy, constant, and terrifying weight against his back. Paranoia was no longer a weakness; it was his armor.

Sujata was a fleeting shadow in the dusk. She had swapped her usual clothes for a loose black hoodie and tattered jeans, her face scrubbed clean of makeup. She was a portrait of urban exhaustion, a woman returning from a long and thankless shift, and it was the perfect disguise. But beneath the performance, her heart was a frantic, silent drum against her ribs. Tucked in her backpack, beneath a decoy bag of stale vada pav, were two small, crudely melted lumps of gold. They were misshapen and impure, looking less like treasure and more like something pulled from the city's gutters. They were perfect.

Dev was the third to arrive, his limp more pronounced tonight, his breath coming in shallow, pained gasps. The bruises on his face had begun to fade to a sickly yellow, a stark contrast to his pale, fiercely determined expression. In his torn hoodie and flapping shoe, he looked utterly bankrupt, a man who had already lost everything. It was the best camouflage a man with a fortune stitched into the inner seam of his shirt could ask for. He gave Rahul and Sujata a single, tight nod, his eyes hard and focused. No words were needed. This wasn't about friendship. This was about the grim, bloody business of survival.

Chung was the last to appear, slipping through the broken door with the unnerving silence of a predator. Her guitar case was slung across her back, a familiar, unremarkable sight in these streets. But she carried it with a new stiffness, her movements sharp and economical, her eyes unsmiling, her mouth a flat, hard line. Inside the case's hidden foam lining, her share of the gold dust lay against the black velvet like a secret, captive galaxy. She set the case down with a slow, deliberate care, as if it contained not just a fortune, but a life she had not yet allowed herself to imagine living.

For a long moment, no one spoke. The silence in the warehouse was absolute, thick with the unspoken prayers of people who had forgotten how to pray. Finally, Rahul knelt, the sound of his knees cracking loud in the quiet. He spread a crumpled piece of paper on the floor—a rough map, sketched in cheap ballpoint pen on the back of an old grocery bill. He tapped five crude circles.

"Five places," he said, his voice low and steady, a general briefing his troops. "Small, local jewelers. Deep in the side streets where the city forgets to look. The kind of places that run on cash and don't have cameras. They don't ask questions." He paused, meeting their anxious gazes. "Usually."

"Usually?" Dev repeated, the word a soft, anxious echo that hung in the air.

Rahul just nodded. "We're improvising," he said simply. The admission was a cold splash of water: they were amateurs playing a professional's game.

"Two teams," Chung cut in, her voice sharp, taking command. "We split up. It halves the risk and draws less attention. One person goes in. One stays outside as lookout. The lookout's only job is to watch. If things go bad, they run. No heroes. No waiting."

"Cash only," Dev added, his voice firm, his mind already running through the potential traps. "No receipts, no names, no paper trail. We don't exist."

"And no greed," Sujata said, her voice quiet but clear, a moral anchor in their sea of desperation. "We take the first fair offer we get. No haggling, no arguing, no pushing our luck. In and out. Fifteen minutes, maximum."

The rules were set, a fragile scaffold of survival built from their collective fear. The silence returned, heavier this time, as they all looked at each other, the unspoken question of who would trust whom hanging between them. Dev's gaze fell on Sujata. He saw the slight, almost imperceptible tremor in her hands as she clutched her backpack strap. He thought of her niece, of the monsters like Vikrant that this city was full of. A fierce, protective instinct, sharp and undeniable, rose in his chest.

"I'll go with Sujata," he said suddenly, his voice so firm it left no room for argument.

Sujata turned to him, her eyes wide with surprise. For a single, long heartbeat, the raw fear in her expression was replaced by something else, something softer. A flicker of profound relief. The rigid, defensive line of her shoulders relaxed, just a fraction, a silent surrender to his offered protection.

Rahul saw the entire, silent exchange, and a small, knowing smile touched his lips. He understood completely. He turned his attention to the last remaining person. "That leaves you and me, Deadbeat Dreamer."

Chung looked him up and down, a flicker of dark amusement in her sharp eyes. "Try to keep up, Uncle," she smirked.

They stood, a silent agreement passing between them. The teams were set. They were two halves of the same broken, desperate coin, about to be tossed into the unforgiving machinery of the city.

The First Sale

They found the shop tucked away in a narrow, suffocating lane where the buildings leaned in so close they seemed to be whispering secrets to each other. The air was thick with the smell of sewage and stale incense. The shop itself was a dusty, cramped vault, its barred window barely distinguishable from the sagging storefronts around it. Inside, a single fluorescent tube flickered erratically, casting a sickly, pale light on a balding man with tobacco-stained fingers. His eyes, small and shrewd, took them in with a single, dismissive glance and then returned to his work. He had already classified them: two broke, desperate nobodies. Perfect.

Sujata moved first. Her heart was a frantic bird trapped against her ribs, but she forced an outward calm she did not feel. Her hands remained steady as she reached into her backpack and placed one of the lumpy, misshapen gold coins on the scratched glass counter.

"Recycled scrap," she said, her voice deliberately low and flat, stripped of all emotion.

The man sighed, the sound of a man infinitely inconvenienced. He picked up the lump without a word, turning it over and over, his expression a mask of profound, professional boredom. He weighed it on a tarnished brass scale, his eyes narrowing just a fraction as the scale dipped lower than he clearly expected. He frowned. "Where did you get this?" he asked, his tone flat and accusatory.

"Family junk," Dev cut in, his voice a little too loud, a little too defensive. "We're clearing out old things. No papers. We just want a quick cash sale."

The man grunted, dropping the lump back onto the counter with a dismissive thud. He named a price. It was a number so offensively low it was a calculated insult, the kind of offer you make to people you assume have no other options. A hot, familiar anger, the same helpless rage he'd felt in the alley, surged through Dev. His fists clenched inside his hoodie pockets. He opened his mouth to protest, but before a single, disastrous word could escape, he felt a light but firm touch on his arm. Sujata. A silent, urgent command: *Don't*. He took a slow, steadying breath, the anger a hot coal behind his teeth.

Sujata leaned forward, a sweet, disarming smile blooming on her face, a smile that didn't come close to reaching her eyes. "Add two thousand to that, uncle," she said, her voice warm and disarmingly friendly. "We were just on our way to see Pappu bhai in the next lane. My friend said he's giving very good rates these days."

It was a complete, audacious bluff, a gamble based on a name she'd heard a street vendor mention once. The jeweler's eyes flickered with irritation. He cursed under his breath, spat a stream of tobacco juice into a bin beside him, and stared at her, his eyes trying to see through her performance. After a long, tense moment of silent calculation, he let out another aggravated sigh and grudgingly counted out the extra two thousand. The deal was done. A thick, grubby wad of notes was pushed into Sujata's hand, and they slipped back out into the humid, neon-lit night.

They ducked into a dark, crooked alley littered with broken crates, their hearts still pounding. The moment they were out of sight, Sujata leaned against the grimy brick wall, and a breathless, disbelieving laugh escaped her. "We did it," she whispered, the words a fragile, triumphant prayer.

Dev stared at her, his anger completely replaced by a stunned admiration. A slow, shy smile, a sight so rare it felt like a miracle in itself, spread across his face. "You're... dangerous," he said, his voice rough with awe.

She nudged his shoulder playfully, a small touch that lingered, charged with the adrenaline of their shared victory. "Stick with me, Wanderwolf," she murmured, her voice soft and inviting. "We might just survive this city together."

In that moment, under the flickering neon glow, Dev looked at her and felt a profound, aching sense of relief.

It wasn't the fiery certainty of romance; it was the quiet, desperate gratitude of a drowning man realizing he is not alone in the endless, churning sea. Their eyes held, and something fragile and reckless sparked between them. He coughed, looking away, a faint blush creeping up his neck. Sujata just smiled to herself. Not all the gold they had found, she realized, was the kind you could weigh on a scale.

The Second Sale

Rahul's hands were slick with sweat inside his pockets. Their second target was a dingy little box wedged between a paan stall, which filled the air with the cloying, sweet scent of betel nut, and a shack selling pirated DVDs, from which the tinny, distorted sounds of a Bollywood action sequence bled into the street. The shop's entrance was little more than a hole in the wall, covered by a thick metal grill, its bars rusted and pitted from decades of monsoon rain.

Inside, a man with a bored, greasy face sat behind the grill, methodically counting a stack of coins. He didn't look up as they approached, a deliberate act of dominance that forced them to stand there in an awkward, vulnerable silence, smelling the paan and listening to the fake gunshots.

"Scrap?" he finally grunted, his eyes still fixed on his coins.

"Yes," Rahul said, his voice coming out a little too high, a little too eager. He slid their small, newspaper-wrapped packet through the narrow slot at the bottom of the grill.

The man let out an exaggerated sigh, as if their business was the greatest inconvenience of his day. He picked up the packet, his movements slow and deliberate. He weighed it in his palm. He sniffed it. He took a dirty file from a drawer and scraped at the metal with a loud, grating sound. "No hallmark," he stated, his voice flat. It was not a question; it was an accusation.

"It's old," Rahul said, his mind racing to remember their rehearsed story. "Family junk."

The man finally looked up. His gaze was cold, deeply suspicious, and utterly devoid of curiosity. He stared at Rahul for a long, uncomfortable moment, then his eyes flicked to Chung, lingering, calculating. In that silence, the air grew thick and heavy. Rahul's heart began to hammer against his ribs, a frantic, trapped bird. He could feel the blood pounding in his ears.

Beside him, he was aware of a subtle shift, a change in the very air. Chung had moved, almost imperceptibly, placing one foot slightly behind his. Her body, which had been relaxed, was now a coiled spring of pure, focused tension. He could feel her readiness, a silent, deadly promise that both terrified and reassured him. She was ready to yank him out of the line of fire.

The jeweler finally named a price. It was low, but it wasn't an insult. It was a fair, take-it-or-leave-it offer from a man who knew they had no other options. Before his own fear could make him hesitate, before he could do anything to arouse more suspicion, Rahul agreed instantly. "Done."

The cash was counted and pushed through the slot. They took it and walked away, forcing themselves to move at a normal, unhurried pace, the feeling of the jeweler's eyes on their backs a physical, prickling weight. They turned the first corner, then a second. Only when they had ducked into the deep, absolute darkness of a back alley did Rahul finally let out the breath he'd been holding in a long, shuddering gasp. A laugh, sharp and slightly hysterical, burst from his lips.

"You move like a panther," he panted, leaning against a wall, his legs weak with relief. He looked at Chung with a new, profound sense of awe. "I felt you get ready back there."

Chung arched a single, unimpressed eyebrow, her face a mask of cool indifference. "And you look like a lost tourist about to be eaten," she replied, her voice completely deadpan.

He laughed harder, a real, helpless, gut-wrenching sound of pure, unadulterated relief. And for the first time, Chung's lips cracked into a small, rare smile. It was a wounded, crooked, and utterly beautiful thing, and in the oppressive darkness of the alley, it felt as bright as any star.

Dev and Sujata were the first to return, slipping back into the warehouse's deep shadows like ghosts. They didn't speak, just sat in the darkness, the wad of cash a hot, unbelievable weight in Sujata's bag, every passing minute stretching into an eternity of anxious waiting. Finally, they heard the soft crunch of footsteps outside. Rahul and Chung appeared in the doorway, their faces pale and strained in the moonlight.

For a long moment, the four of them just stood there, breathing in the dusty, familiar air of their sanctuary, a silent, four-way confirmation that they had all made it back alive. Then, with a shared, unspoken agreement, they moved to the center of the room. One by one, they emptied their pockets, their bags, their satchels. Two thick, grubby wads of cash landed on the concrete floor, a fortune that smelled of sweat, fear, and the city's grime.

They stared at the pile of money. It was real. The plan, born of desperation and whispered in fear, had actually worked. A sound, half-sob and half-laugh, escaped Rahul's lips. It was a sound of pure, unadulterated relief, and it broke the spell. A moment later, Dev was laughing too, a deep, joyous sound that was utterly alien to the grim walls of the warehouse. Sujata joined in, her laughter light and breathless, and finally, even Chung let out a sharp, surprised bark of a laugh.

The city howled and snarled outside, but inside their small, dusty circle, there was only the sound of their shared, impossible victory. The gold was real. The plan was real. The fragile, trembling promise of a different life was no longer a dream. It was lying right there on the floor in front of them. And as they finally settled into a comfortable, exhausted silence, something even rarer and more precious began to take root in the broken ground of their world. Friendship. Family. And in the quiet, shared glances between them, the first, tentative shoots of love.

CHAPTER TEN

Shadows at the Edge

Tonight, the warehouse smelled different. The usual scent of damp concrete and rust was still present, but woven through it now was the faint, papery smell of cash and the unmistakable, sweet aroma of hope. In the center of their circle, illuminated by the warm, flickering glow of a single salvaged lantern, sat a messy, beautiful pile of money. It wasn't the neat, crisp stacks from the movies; it was a chaotic mound of sweaty, crumpled notes, bound in rough bundles with cheap rubber bands and bits of string. It was real. And it was enough.

For a long time, no one spoke. They just stared at the pile, the soft light casting long, dancing shadows on their exhausted faces. They were savoring the quiet, dizzying feeling of having gambled against the entire city and, for the first time in their collective lives, having actually won.

Finally, Rahul leaned back against a rusted pillar, the metal groaning under his weight. He let out a deep, shuddering sigh, a sound that seemed to carry with it the weight of a thousand silent humiliations and a lifetime of quiet disappointment. "We could actually do this," he said, his voice soft with a disbelief he couldn't quite hide.

Sujata smiled, a small, private expression, as she traced an invisible pattern in the dust with her finger. "Not just survive," she murmured, the words a quiet promise to Anaya, to her sister, and to herself. "Actually live."

Chung let out a soft snort and tossed a crumpled, empty chips packet, which bounced harmlessly off Rahul's knee. "Don't get soft now, Uncle," she teased, though her voice lacked its usual sharp, cynical edge. "Dreams cost extra, you know."

Dev chuckled, a low, breathless sound. A nervous, hopeful energy was buzzing under his skin, making it impossible to sit still. He leaned forward, his eyes bright. "Do you think... maybe we could start something real?" he asked, the words shy and clumsy. "All of us? Together?"

"Like a business?" Sujata asked, her head tilting with a genuine, thoughtful interest that made Dev's heart skip a beat.

"Like an art and music school for street kids and other delinquents?" Chung deadpanned, though her eyes held a flicker of something that was not a joke at all.

A wide, genuine grin, the kind he hadn't worn in years, spread across Rahul's face. "A bike courier company," he said, the old, bitter fantasy now feeling solid and real on his tongue. "We'll call it Starfall Couriers."

The absurd, beautiful, and utterly perfect name floated in the dusty air between them. And then they laughed. It wasn't the harsh, brittle laughter of survival. It was a deep, rolling, belly-aching laughter, the kind that scrubs out fear and leaves you feeling light and breathless. For a few perfect, golden moments, the city and all its dangers, all its cruelties, simply ceased to exist. There were only the four of them, the flickering lantern, and the impossible, beautiful, and terrifying possibility of a different life. But dreams, especially the ones forged in desperation, are fragile things, and in the dark corners of the city, other plans were already in motion.

Meanwhile...

In a foul-smelling bar in Kurla East, where the constant rumble of passing trains rattled the grimy windows, Vikrant ground out his cigarette in a cracked, overflowing ashtray. He absently touched his temple, the spot still tender from where Sujata had shoved him. The incident hadn't just cost him his job; it had made him a laughingstock among his peers. As he stewed in his own bitter humiliation, he overheard a hushed conversation from two scrap dealers at the next table—whispers of strange, unrefined "fire gold" appearing in the back-alley markets, sold by nervous, desperate-looking people.

Vikrant's head snapped up. His predator's instinct, honed by a lifetime of sniffing out weakness and opportunity, flared to life. The timing was too perfect. The location, near the slums she frequented, was too coincidental. It had to be her. Stupid, lucky Sujata had stumbled into something big. A thin, cruel smile stretched his lips. His plans for revenge, which had been about simple, brutal payback, now blossomed into something far grander. She wasn't just going to pay him what she owed him anymore. She was going to pay him everything.

And Elsewhere...

In a dusty, forgotten office of the Geological Survey, surrounded by towering stacks of forgotten files, Inspector D'Souza leaned back in his creaking chair. The official inquiry into the "unexplained seismic event" had been stamped, filed, and officially closed. Budget constraints. Lack of conclusive evidence. But D'Souza was a man who hated loose ends and smelled opportunity in the laziness of his superiors. He pulled the physical files: the blurry seismic printouts, the dismissed eyewitness accounts from a handful of late-night pilots, and a decades-old survey map of the city's industrial outskirts.

With a ruler and a red pen, he methodically cross-referenced the timeline with the reported coordinates. The lines converged on a single, precise point: the abandoned textile mill grounds. Unreported meteor strikes, he knew from experience, always meant one thing: scavengers. And scavengers meant a mess that a clever officer could clean up, for a price. He tapped his pen on the hand-drawn map of the area, a single, sharp red circle marking the probable impact zone. He would make a quiet, off-the-books visit tomorrow. Before the bureaucracy could get in the way. Before whatever had fallen was lost to the city's rats.

Back in the fragile, lantern-lit safety of the warehouse, drunk on a possibility they hadn't allowed themselves to feel in years, they began to build castles in the air.

"I'm quitting my job," Rahul announced, the words feeling both terrifying and thrilling as he spoke them aloud.

Sujata looked up, her expression a mixture of sharp worry and dawning excitement. "Are you sure? Is that wise?"

"Not tomorrow," he said, a real, unforced smile tugging at his lips. "I'm not an idiot. But soon. I am done crawling for a woman who despises me." He leaned forward into the light, his eyes alight with an idea that had been a bitter, impossible fantasy just days ago. "I'm going to start my own delivery service. Starfall Couriers. Just a few second-hand bikes. We know the back alleys better than anyone. We'll be faster and cheaper than the big guys. No middlemen, no corporate nonsense, just us."

"Man, I'd work for you in a heartbeat!" Dev said, his enthusiasm immediate and genuine, the words tumbling out of him.

"You don't even own a bike," Chung teased, though her tone was surprisingly gentle.

"I'll buy one!" Dev shot back, his grin wide and hopeful. "With my share!"

Sujata leaned back against a pillar, a dreamy, faraway look in her eyes. "If you start a courier company," she said, her voice soft, "I'll open a small café. Right next door to your office. A place for your delivery boys to rest. For anyone in the neighborhood who needs a good cup of cutting chai and a hot vada pav."

Rahul stared at her, completely stunned. The idea of his own office was one thing; the idea of it being a place someone else would choose to build beside was another entirely. "You'd trust me?" he asked, his voice suddenly hoarse. "With your money? With your own dream?"

She met his gaze, her smile worn but radiant in the lantern light. "I trusted you enough to dig through hell with me, Rahul," she said simply.

The words landed with a quiet force that humbled him more than any insult ever had. For a single, perfect moment, their stupid, impossible dreams felt real. They were no longer just fantasies; they were anchors, punching strong, deep roots into the hard, broken soil of the city.

Suddenly, the sharp, violent buzz of a phone vibrated against the concrete floor, the sound a physical shock in the quiet room.

The laughter died instantly. The warm, hopeful atmosphere evaporated, sucked out of the room and replaced by a sudden, familiar, and bone-deep cold. They all froze, their bodies instantly returning to the coiled, high-alert posture of prey. In their world, an unexpected call at this hour was never good news. Dev, whose phone it was, reached for it slowly, as if it were a venomous snake. He didn't answer. He just turned the brightly lit screen toward the others.

Unknown Number...

No name. No location. Just a blank, anonymous, and deeply menacing threat.

"Ignore it," Rahul said, his voice flat and hard, all the warmth gone from it. "It's probably a wrong number."

But they all knew it wasn't. It was a crack in the thin wall of their secret world. It was a reminder that fortune is never free and that the city was always, always listening. The first seed of a new, colder fear had been planted. Slowly, without another word, they began to pack up their cash, their movements no longer giddy with success, but careful, reverent, and deeply, deeply afraid.

CHAPTER ELEVEN

FIRST STEPS, FRAGILE STEPS

The morning after a miracle feels unnervingly normal. The city woke just as it always did—not with a gentle dawn, but with the shriek of a train and the clatter of a thousand steel shutters. It was the same hostile symphony they had always known, but for the first time, it sounded different. It was the sound of a world they had just cheated, a world that was still oblivious to the impossible secret tucked away in four separate, shabby rooms. For the four souls who had touched a piece of a fallen star, this particular morning was dragging a reality back that was sharper, heavier, and far more dangerous than anything they had known before.

Rahul — The First Flight

Rahul stood across the street, watching the squat glass building that had served as his prison for three long years. The faded blue sign, *Infix Solutions Pvt. Ltd.*, seemed to sag under the weight of the city's grime, a tired monument to his own quiet failures. He remembered the hundreds of times he had pushed through those greasy glass doors with his head bowed, a man bracing for the daily, soul-crushing blows of indifference and contempt. But today, as he stared at the familiar, hated facade, the building looked different. Smaller. Flimsier. Made of glass and lies. The building hadn't changed; the power it held over him had simply vanished. He straightened his back, a small, conscious movement that felt like a tectonic shift within him, a quiet revolution.

The resignation letter, saved as a draft in his old email account, was a promise. But the true source of his courage was the memory of the heavy, glittering dust hidden in his flat. It was a constant, secret hum beneath the surface of his old life, a tangible anchor of worth that whispered promises of freedom and dignity. For the first time in his adult life, the future no longer looked like a solid, unbreachable wall. It looked like an open window.

He was turning to leave when a sharp, familiar, and mocking voice sliced through the humid air.

"Leaving early again, Rahul? Can't say I'm surprised."

He stopped. He turned slowly, deliberately. It was Meghna Shroff, holding court in the designated smoking area, a cigarette in one hand, a coffee mug in the other. She was flanked by her usual sycophantic interns, her audience for this small, casual act of cruelty. The old Rahul would have flinched, his eyes dropping to the pavement as he stammered an excuse. But the old Rahul was a ghost, a victim left for dead on an unfinished bridge. This new Rahul met her gaze directly, and for the first time, he did not look away. A slow, calm smile spread across his face, an expression so foreign to this context that it was an act of aggression. It was not the polite, submissive smile of an employee. It was the calm, unreadable smile of a man who held a winning hand.

"Yes, Meghna," he said, his voice quiet but carrying an unfamiliar, steady weight that cut through the street noise.

"I am leaving." He held her gaze, letting the silence stretch, and saw the first flicker of confusion in her eyes. She had been expecting a cower, and he had given her a challenge.

"And soon," he added softly, letting the words land with a quiet precision, "you'll be talking to my back forever."

Her poisonous smirk faltered. It was just for a fraction of a second, a tiny, almost imperceptible tightening at the corner of her mouth, a brief loss of condescending power in her eyes. But he saw it. It was the crack in the armor of a bully who has just realized her victim is no longer afraid. And it felt more satisfying, more profoundly victorious, than any promotion ever could have.

Without waiting for a reply, he turned his back on her—the ultimate, final dismissal—and walked away. He didn't hurry. He caught his reflection in the greasy window of a closed storefront and paused. For a second, the stooped, invisible clerk stared back, his eyes still clouded with thirty years of 'yes-ma'ams.' Rahul blinked, straightening his spine until the ghost vanished, replaced by a man who no longer needed to look away. He walked with an even, measured pace, feeling the phantom weight of invisible wings beginning to unfurl from his tired, aching shoulders, ready, finally, to fly.

Sujata—A Taste of Freedom

Sujata stood on the crowded pavement, a still point in the chaotic stream of pedestrians. Her eyes were fixed on a tiny, shuttered storefront, a forgotten space squeezed between a laundry shop that bled the smell of bleach into the air and a defunct PCO booth covered in peeling movie posters. The shop's paint was flaking, its metal shutters were dented and rusted, and it looked like one strong monsoon might finally wash it away. To anyone else, it was a ruin. To Sujata, it was a kingdom waiting to be born.

She stepped closer, pressing her forehead against the cool, grimy glass of the window. The decay vanished. In her mind, the grimy walls became a cheerful, vibrant yellow. The scent of bleach was replaced by the aroma of fresh cutting chai, ginger, and cardamom, mingling with the spicy sizzle of poha on a hot pan. She could hear the clatter of clean cups on saucers, the murmur of happy customers, and, above it all, the sound of Anaya's carefree laughter from a small, sunlit corner filled with secondhand books and coloring pencils. *Scarlet Café*. The name bloomed in her mind, a stubborn, beautiful flower determined to grow in the city's cracks. "One day," she whispered to her reflection in the dirty glass, the words not a wish but a solemn, unbreakable vow.

Later that afternoon, she walked toward the hospital. Her steps were lighter, imbued with a purpose that felt new and exhilarating. The old, familiar fear was still there, a cold knot in her stomach, but it was no longer all-consuming. It was a manageable shadow, held at bay by the bright, fierce light of her new, tangible hope. That hope, however, faltered the moment she pushed through the heavy hospital doors. The smell of antiseptic—cold, sterile, and unforgiving—instantly replaced the warm, hopeful scent of her imaginary café, a harsh reminder of the world she was still fighting.

In the pediatric ward, Anaya was a small, vibrant sun in a vast, sterile universe. She sat up in her bed, the thin oxygen tubes at her nose bobbing with every restless kick of her legs, a notebook clutched in her hands. Her face lit up the moment she saw Sujata, a smile so pure it was a physical blow to the heart.

"Aunty Su!" she squealed, waving a crayon-scribbled page with triumphant energy.

Sujata's own heart clenched with a love so fierce it was painful. She knelt by the bed, taking the offered drawing. It was a small, bright house, bursting with gloriously crooked windows and a disproportionate number of bright red hearts. "Is this our house?" Sujata asked, her throat tightening, the words thick with unshed tears.

Anaya nodded solemnly, her eyes wide and deadly serious. "And you're the queen, Aunty Su."

A sound that was half-laugh, half-sob tore from Sujata's lips. A queen. Her. A queen of cheap bars and secret, desperate transactions, a queen who sold pieces of a fallen star to keep her kingdom of two alive. The title was so absurd and so perfect it broke something open inside her. She pulled Anaya into a careful, fierce hug, burying her face in the little girl's hair, breathing in the simple, clean scent of her. She would build this little girl a world where queens didn't have to bleed for every scrap of hope. She would build it with her own two hands, one brick and one cup of chai at a time.

Chung—New Chords

Chung walked the cracked streets of Mahim with no destination. The guitar case, with its secret, heavy lining, felt less like an instrument and more like a ball and chain bumping against her back with every step. Her apartment, once a sanctuary, now felt like a tomb, haunted by a ghost she had created. She wasn't hunting for a gig. She wasn't bracing for the jeers of drunks. She was simply adrift, a ghost in her own city, a prisoner of a treasure she couldn't spend and a freedom she didn't know how to use. She found herself watching the city's other ghosts: the children. The ones who darted between cars at traffic lights, their small hands selling cheap plastic toys, their eyes old with a weariness that had no business being in a child's face.

Near a paan shop, she saw two of them. A boy of about eight with a fiercely protective gaze that was far too old for him and a little girl who clung to his hand, her face smudged with a familiar city grime. Their cheap rubber sandals were held together with knotted rubber bands. They weren't begging; they were simply watching the world with a silent, wary, and calculating intensity that Chung recognized instantly. It was the look of a survivor.

On an impulse she didn't fully understand, she stopped. She knelt on the pavement, her movements slow and deliberate, the way one might approach a feral cat. She unslung her guitar. The children watched her, their bodies instantly tensing, ready to flee at the first sign of a threat.

"You want to make some noise?" she asked, her voice softer than she intended.

The boy just stared, his expression a battlefield of deep, ingrained suspicion and a single, flickering spark of childish curiosity. The little girl hid behind his leg. Chung didn't push. Instead, a rare, mischievous grin touched her lips. She plugged the guitar into the tiny, battery-powered amplifier clipped to her belt, cranked the gain to maximum, and ripped into a loud, distorted, bluesy riff. It was a messy, angry, and unapologetically alive sound that screamed through the evening air. The paan shop owner jumped and let out a string of curses.

And the boy laughed. It wasn't a giggle; it was a real, sudden, joyful bark of a laugh. The little girl peeked out from behind him, her eyes wide, and clapped her hands. They were hooked.

Within minutes, three more children had drifted over, drawn not by a pretty melody, but by the raw, honest, and unapologetic noise. Chung sat cross-legged on the dirty pavement, the city's chaos fading into a distant hum. She showed them how to hold the guitar, how to make a single string scream, and how to beat a defiant rhythm on the wooden body. For the first time in a long, long time, she was playing not for money, not for survival, but for the simple, pure, and explosive joy of creation. In their bright, hungry, and intelligent eyes, she saw not victims to be saved, but fellow artists. Maybe she couldn't save the city, and maybe she couldn't even save herself. But she could share a chord. She could start there.

Dev—New Wheels

The dealership was a graveyard of old dreams, rows of aging motorcycles packed tightly together under a tin roof. The air was thick with the smell of grease, petrol, and rust. Dev's fingers trembled as he counted out the thick, worn wad of cash onto the greasy counter. Each note felt impossibly heavy, a small piece of a life he had never, ever spent on himself. The salesman, a bored man with oil-stained fingernails, didn't even look at him. He simply recounted the money with the practiced, dismissive speed of a man who saw a hundred desperate faces like Dev's every week, then shoved a faded carbon receipt and a set of rusted keys toward him.

Dev picked them up. And there it was. His. A battered, second-hand Honda CD 110 Dream, its black paint scratched, its front mudguard dented. One of the side mirrors was missing, leaving an empty, threaded hole. It was imperfect. It was scarred. It was a survivor. It was, he thought, just like him. And it was paid for. Not with a loan, not with begged money, but with a piece of a fallen star.

He swung his leg over the seat, his movements slow and almost reverent. He ran a hand along the worn, sun-cracked rubber of the handlebars. This was not just a machine. This was the end of two-hour, soul-crushing walks through garbage-choked lanes. This was dignity. This was time. This was freedom. He put the key in the ignition, his heart hammering in his chest, and gave it a turn. The engine sputtered once, a pathetic, dying cough. He tried again. It coughed, then sputtered, and then, with a deep, rattling, and gloriously loud roar, it came to life beneath him.

A laugh—loud, unrestrained, and slightly hysterical—burst from Dev's lips. It was a broken, joyous, beautiful sound that startled a passing rickshaw driver. "I'm coming for you, world," he whispered, a grin stretching his face as he gripped the handlebars tighter. "And this time, I'm bringing friends."

But as Dev took his first, triumphant taste of freedom, the storm clouds that had been gathering on the horizon finally began to move. In a smoke-filled backroom, Vikrant listened to an informant on a burner phone, a cruel, shark-like smile spreading across his face as the man described a woman seen meeting strange men near the old mill grounds. And in a cramped government office, Inspector D'Souza polished his badge, his eyes fixed on the red-circled anomaly on his map. He had a location. He had whispers of a strange transaction. Now, all he needed were names. Tomorrow, he would start asking the kind of questions that tear dreams apart. For this one, perfect, fleeting night, the city belonged to four fragile hopes, lit by the dangerous, defiant belief that they could win. They had no idea it was already too late.

OF BROKEN HEARTS AND HUNTING DOGS

Tonight, the warehouse felt different. It was less like a hideout and more like a home. They had gathered not to plan or to sell, but because the thought of being alone in their small, silent rooms, with only their fears for company, had become unbearable. Here, in the dusty, shared quiet, they felt safe.

They sprawled on the concrete floor in an easy, comfortable circle, a small, makeshift family in a vast, industrial cathedral. Rahul was hunched over a flattened cigarette carton, completely absorbed in sketching logos for "Starfall Couriers." He drew swooping arrows and winged packages, his brow furrowed in a concentration so intense it was almost comical, a man trying to build a future with a cheap, leaking pen.

Across from him, Chung wasn't playing the angry, distorted riffs she used as armor on the streets. She was plucking a slow, surprisingly gentle melody, the clean, sad notes filling the vast, empty space with a fragile, hesitant beauty. It was the sound of a wall slowly, carefully being taken down, brick by brick.

Sujata sat cross-legged, her focus entirely on the colorful bracelet she was weaving from thin strips of discarded fabric. Her fingers moved with a steady, meditative rhythm, a quiet, determined act of creating something whole and beautiful from the city's broken scraps.

Dev watched her from across the circle, a battered thermos of chai sitting forgotten beside him. He was mesmerized not just by the graceful, efficient movement of her hands, but by the profound stillness she radiated. He knew, with a certainty that ached in his own chest, some of the hell she had been through. Yet she sat there, not as a victim, but as an artist, a woman who refused to be defined by her scars. A warmth bloomed in his chest that was both terrifying and wonderful, an emotion so new and powerful it almost made him dizzy.

After a while, Chung's soft melody faded into a final, lingering chord. She stood up, stretching her arms above her head. "I need some air," she announced to no one in particular, slinging her guitar over her shoulder.

A few minutes later, Rahul, having exhausted his artistic inspiration for the moment, got to his feet as well. "I'll just... check the perimeter," he muttered, the old, paranoid excuse now sounding flimsy and slightly ridiculous even to his own ears. He gave Dev a quick, almost imperceptible nod—a silent, brotherly gesture of understanding—and followed Chung out into the night.

And just like that, the vast warehouse fell silent. The city hummed and rumbled outside, a distant, sleeping beast. But inside, there was only the soft, steady sound of two people breathing in the dark, the space between them no longer a minefield of suspicion, but charged with something new, tender, and unspoken.

A long, comfortable silence settled between them, a quiet so profound he could hear the faint hiss of the lantern. The question he wanted to ask was a dangerous weight in his chest. It felt intrusive, cruel, but a part of him, the part that was beginning to care for her in a way that scared him, needed to know. He cleared his throat, the sound small in the vast, dark space.

"Can I ask you something?" he said, his voice barely a whisper.

Sujata looked up from her weaving, a quiet, questioning look in her eyes. "Sure."

He fumbled for the words, his gaze dropping to the dusty floor. "That night... at the bar," he began, then trailed off, a flush of shame creeping up his neck. "Your boss... what he said..."

A sad, knowing smile touched Sujata's lips. She didn't need him to finish. She carefully set her half-finished bracelet aside and leaned back against the concrete pillar, her gaze becoming distant. "You want to know if I slept with him for money," she said, her voice quiet and steady, robbing the question of its intended ugliness with her own direct honesty.

"No, I just..." Dev started, desperate to backtrack, to take back the clumsy intrusion. But she held up a hand, stopping him.

"It's okay," she said softly. "You deserve to know the truth." She took a deep, steadying breath. "Yes. I did what I had to do. For Anaya. For her medicines, for the doctor's fees that were piling up. For another month of hope. It wasn't a choice between right and wrong. It was a choice between my pride and her next breath." She shrugged, a small, brittle gesture that spoke of immense pain. "It's not something I'm proud of. But I'm not ashamed of it either. To keep her alive, I would have done worse."

Dev listened, and something deep inside his own bruised heart shifted. He wasn't hearing a confession of shame. He was hearing a warrior describe a brutal battle she had fought and won. He thought of his own unending sacrifices, the endless stream of money for a wedding he wasn't truly a part of, the physical beating he had taken for a laptop that wasn't even his. He understood, with a clarity that was both painful and beautiful, the impossible choices made for love.

He swallowed against a sudden thickness in his throat. "I don't think less of you for it," he said, his voice hoarse with an emotion he couldn't name. "I think... you might be the strongest person I have ever met."

Sujata blinked slowly, her hard-won composure finally cracking. Her breath hitched. No one, in her entire life, had ever said anything like that to her. The judgment of others, both spoken and unspoken, had been a constant, suffocating presence. She bit her lip, hard, fighting against the sudden, sharp sting of tears.

"I know what it's like," Dev continued, his own voice low and raw with shared experience. "To have to choose between two impossible options. To have to give up pieces of yourself just to keep the people you love whole."

Sujata looked at him then, truly looked at him, and saw past the fresh stitches and the worn-out clothes. She saw the battered, stubborn goodness in him, a quiet decency that this city should have crushed and devoured long ago. A slow, shy, and utterly real smile bloomed on her face.

"Thanks, Wanderwolf," she whispered, the silly codename now feeling like the most intimate of titles.

He smiled back, a clumsy, boyish grin that was achingly sweet. For a long, perfect moment, the debts, the dangers, and the city itself faded away into a distant, muffled hum, leaving just two broken people, finally seeing each other, and themselves, as whole.

Meanwhile, Outside...

Chung leaned against the cool, crumbling brick of the outer wall, her gaze fixed on the handful of faint, stubborn stars that had managed to burn through the city's yellow haze. A few feet away, Rahul stood with his hands shoved deep in his pockets, the posture of a man trying to look casual and failing. The silence between them was long and comfortable, punctuated only by the distant wail of a train and the low hum of the highway. He passed her the cheap bidi they were sharing.

"You're different than I expected," she said, looking at him sideways as she exhaled a stream of smoke.

"Different how?"

"Less... pathetic," she said with a smirk.

He laughed, a deep, genuine sound that surprised them both. "You're different too," he countered. "Less... feral."

She shrugged, the smirk softening into something more vulnerable. "It's easier not to bite the world when you're not fighting it alone," she admitted quietly. He fumbled for a topic that wasn't about gold or fear.

"The guitar," he said. "Why music?"

She hitched the strap of her guitar higher on her shoulder. "Strings don't lie," she said, her voice quiet and hard. "You play an A chord, it sounds like an A. You bend a string, it screams. It does exactly what you tell it to, every time. People... people are not so reliable."

He nodded slowly, the simple, brutal truth of her words settling deep in his bones. "I lied to myself for years," he heard himself admit, the confession escaping before he could stop it. "Told myself my job wasn't so bad. That letting my boss humiliate me was just 'paying my dues.' That I was lucky to even have a job to complain about."

Chung turned her head, looking at him properly for the first time. Her gaze was sharp, analytical, but it held a surprising lack of judgment. "No one," she said, her voice low but fierce, "deserves to be made to feel small just for existing."

Her words hit him with the force of both a slap and a balm. For the first time in what felt like a lifetime, he felt truly seen.

Then, she did something that shocked him more than anything that had happened since the sky fell. She let out a slow, weary sigh and leaned forward, resting her forehead against his chest for a single, fleeting heartbeat. It wasn't a romantic gesture. It was the profound, exhausted gesture of a soldier finally allowing herself a moment of rest against the armor of a trusted comrade. Then she straightened up, taking the bidi from his hand as if nothing had happened. But it had.

As the Night Deepened...

The fragile connections forming in and around the warehouse were a temporary shield against a city that was actively beginning to hunt. In a smoky, greasy cybercafé on SV Road, Vikrant hunched over a sticky keyboard, his eyes burning as he clicked through hours of pirated security camera footage. Frame after grainy frame. Street after blurry street. And then—he stopped. He zoomed in. There. Sujata. Walking with that same stubborn, proud stride he hated, carrying a battered backpack. And next to her, a man he didn't recognize, his posture protective. A sneer twisted Vikrant's lips. *Found you, bitch.* He tapped the keyboard, saving the screenshots to a grimy pen drive.

At that same time, Inspector D'Souza stood in the profound, eerie silence of the abandoned textile estate. He was dressed in plainclothes, his presence a small, methodical disturbance in the night. His flashlight beam swept slowly, patiently, across the scorched earth. He knelt at the edge of the crater, a place that still felt wrong, the air still holding a faint, metallic tang. He ran a gloved hand through the dirt, lifting it to the beam. It glittered. Not mica. Not glass. Something else. Unreported. Unclaimed. He carefully scooped a sample into a small plastic bag and tucked it into his pocket. The gears in his mind were already turning, cold and sharp and inevitable. The hunt was on. Their beautiful, fragile beginnings were already living on borrowed time. The dogs had caught the scent.

CRACKS IN THE CIRCLE

The warehouse was cold tonight, a cold that had nothing to do with the weather. The easy, hopeful camaraderie of the previous nights had completely evaporated, replaced by a brittle, unspoken tension that was as thick as the dust in the air. They had arrived one by one, their greetings clipped, their movements wary. The anonymous phone call had been a stone tossed into the still waters of their hope, and the chilling ripples were now washing over them.

And Sujata was late.

Fifteen minutes. In a city where a lifetime could be decided in the space between heartbeats, fifteen minutes was an eternity of doubt. Rahul paced back and forth, the scuff of his worn sneakers on the concrete the only sound, a frantic, anxious rhythm. *She ran,* a cynical voice in his head whispered. *Of course she ran.* Dev sat with his back pressed against a pillar, his gaze fixed on the empty doorway, his jaw clenched so tightly it ached. Chung sat perfectly still, a statue of pure, cold vigilance, her silence more unnerving than any of Rahul's restless movements.

When Sujata finally appeared in the doorway, breathless and flushed, three pairs of eyes snapped to her with an almost violent intensity.

"Traffic?" Rahul asked, his voice a tight, casual wire that fooled no one.

Sujata nodded, her gaze flickering away from his, unable to meet the force of their collective stare. A cheap, new backpack—not her usual battered purse—was slung over her shoulder. "Sorry," she panted, letting the bag drop to the floor with a heavy, definitive thud. "The hospital visit with Anaya ran late. And I had to dodge a few nosy neighbors on the way out."

The excuse was plausible. Perfect, even. But in the superheated atmosphere of their paranoia, it did nothing to cool the tension. It only added fuel. Chung's sharp, analytical gaze was fixed not on Sujata's face, but on the new backpack. A new bag. After one successful sale. The math was simple. It was brutal. It was, in her world, inevitable.

They settled into their usual circle, but the space between them was no longer a zone of comfort. It was a battlefield of unspoken accusations.

It was Chung who finally gave voice to the ugly, squirming thought they were all having. She looked not at Sujata but at the new backpack lying on the floor.

"So," she began, her voice deceptively light, almost conversational, which made the words infinitely more poisonous. "No one's been tempted? No one's thought about maybe taking their share and making a run for it? Selling a little extra on the side to buy, say, a new bag?"

The question sliced through the room with the force of a physical blow. Rahul went rigid. Dev's head snapped up, a look of pure, wounded disbelief on his face as he looked from Chung to Sujata. And Sujata... Sujata just froze, her face a mask of pure, stunned shock. A sound escaped her lips, a high, brittle, and horrifyingly hollow laugh that echoed in the cavernous space.

"Seriously?" she gasped, her voice trembling with a mixture of raw anger and profound hurt. "After everything we've been through? After everything I told you? You think I would do that?"

"Just asking," Chung said, holding up her hands in a gesture of mock surrender that was anything but apologetic. "Better to clear the air."

But the air wasn't clear. It was now thick and sour with a suspicion that, once spoken aloud, could never truly be taken back.

For a long, brittle moment, the fragile thing they had built—the friendship stitched together from shared hunger and the desperate honesty of their confessions—threatened to turn to dust and blow away. The only sound in the warehouse was their own shallow, ragged breathing.

It was Dev who finally broke the standoff. With a sharp, decisive movement, he reached into his hoodie pocket, pulled out the crumpled wad of cash from the sale, and tossed it into the center of their circle. The bills landed on the dusty concrete with a soft, accusing slap. It was not a gesture of peace. It was a challenge. *Show me.*

Rahul's heart hammered against his ribs. His hand, already deep in his own pocket, tightened around his share of the cash. An ugly, practical voice, the voice of a lifetime of being cheated and dismissed, slithered into his mind. *Hold some back. Just a few notes. They'll never know. How do you know they're not doing the same? Don't be a fool, Rahul. Not again.* The thought was slick and easy, a survival instinct the city had trained into his very bones.

But then he saw Sujata. Her face was a mask of wounded pride, her hands trembling with fury as she unzipped her new backpack. With a jerky, almost violent motion, she pulled out her money and slapped it down hard on top of Dev's. It was not an act of trust; it was an act of defiance. Then he saw Chung. Her jaw was clenched, and she deliberately tilted her guitar case, just enough for the heavy, muffled clink of her hidden gold to be audible to them all—a silent, dangerous proof of her own integrity, and a warning.

He finally looked at Dev, who was watching him, only him. Dev's expression was not trusting. It was simply waiting. He was giving Rahul the choice to be the man he claimed to be or the man the city had tried to make him. In that moment, a wave of profound self-loathing washed over Rahul. He hated that his first instinct was to betray them. He hated that this city had so thoroughly trained him to expect the worst in everyone. With a surge of shame so hot it felt like a fever, he pulled his own wad of cash from his pocket and shoved it angrily into the pile, as if trying to physically cast out his own worst impulses.

"It's all there," he said, his voice quiet and rough with self-disgust.

Sujata met his eyes, and in her gaze, he saw not gratitude, but a shared, weary wariness that mirrored his own. Chung gave a single, sharp nod, a gesture that conceded the moment but promised nothing for the future. They were still together. For now. But the crack had been made, and they all knew, with a certainty that was as cold as the concrete beneath them, that cracks in a foundation never stay small.

Later that night...

The walk home from the warehouse was a special kind of torment. The brittle, splintered trust of the group had left her feeling raw and exposed. Every shadow in the narrow, twisting lanes seemed to stretch and shift, taking on a vaguely human form. The slap of her own sneakers on the wet pavement echoed back at her, sounding unnervingly like a second, heavier set of footsteps. A primal itch crawled at the back of her neck, the old, familiar feeling of being watched, of being hunted. *"It's just the stress,"* she told herself, the poison of Chung's suspicion clouding her mind. But she quickened her pace anyway, her purse clutched tight to her chest.

She was turning into the final, poorly lit alley before her building when a shape detached itself from the deeper shadows. Before she could even process it, a hand—hard, cold, and brutally familiar—clamped over her mouth, stifling her scream. Another arm snaked around her waist like a band of steel, yanking her backward. A voice, thick with the stench of cheap whiskey and pure, undiluted rage, drawled into her ear.

"Miss me?"

Ice flooded her veins. *Vikrant.*

He spun her around and slammed her back against the grimy, wet brick wall, the impact knocking the air from her lungs. His face was inches from hers, his eyes wild and bloodshot. 'You really think you can hide from me, Sujata?' he hissed, his grip on her arms bruisingly tight. He glanced down at the new backpack she was carrying, a sneer twisting his lips. 'Bought yourself something pretty with your dirty money? You think a few new rupees can wash you clean?'"

"Let go of me," she snarled, struggling against him, but he was stronger, fueled by a vicious, proprietary rage that saw her not as a person but as a possession.

"Not until you remember where you belong," he sneered, his foul, hot breath washing over her face.

In that moment, something inside her snapped. The fear didn't vanish, but it was consumed by a pure, white-hot fury that was colder and more dangerous than any fear she had ever felt. She stopped struggling, her body going still, and her eyes darted around, her mind a cold, quick catalog of potential weapons. Her gaze landed on a vendor's large, steel thermos sitting abandoned on a nearby crate.

Without a second of hesitation, she drove her knee, hard, into his groin. He grunted, his grip loosening for a fraction of a second—all the opening she needed. She lunged, grabbing the heavy thermos. She didn't throw it. She swung it with all her strength, a desperate, whistling arc of steel that connected with the side of his head with a sickening, wet thud.

The cap flew off, and a spray of scalding hot chai exploded across his face and chest. He screamed—a raw, animal howl of pure shock and agony—stumbling back, his hands flying to his burning skin.

Sujata didn't wait to see more. She ran. She bolted down the alley, her heart jackhammering against her ribs, shoving past the few stunned onlookers who had emerged from the shadows. She ran until her lungs burned and her legs screamed, not stopping, not even looking back, until she reached the familiar, shadowy gate of the abandoned mill grounds. She collapsed behind it, her body wracked with violent, uncontrollable tremors, gasping for air. She was free. For now.

She pressed her forehead against the cold, rusted metal, fighting back a wave of nausea. She would not cry. She would not scream. And she would not tell the others. Their new, fragile trust had almost shattered tonight over a cheap backpack. She couldn't, she wouldn't, be the one to show up with fresh wounds and more trouble, proving their worst suspicions right. This secret, this new, ugly, and victorious scar, would be hers alone to carry.

CHAPTER FOURTEEN

SHADOWS OVER THE RUINS

It had become a nervous, obsessive ritual. Every night, before heading to the relative safety of the main warehouse, Rahul and Chung would take a long, looping path through the ruins, ending up on the roof of a derelict warehouse that overlooked the crash site. They called it "checking the perimeter," a grim joke that felt less funny with each passing night. Tonight, the air was cold, and the silence around the estate felt heavier, more watchful, as if the land itself was holding its breath.

They were halfway up a rusted, groaning fire escape when Chung suddenly froze, her body going rigid. She didn't speak; she just pointed. Down below, in the heart of the field, a single, sharp beam of light was cutting through the darkness. It wasn't the frantic, scattered light of a scavenger. It was moving with a slow, deliberate, methodical purpose. They exchanged a look of pure, cold dread and scrambled the rest of the way to the roof, their movements now silent and desperate.

They crawled on their bellies across the gritty concrete, the rough surface scraping their hands, until they reached the edge of a crumbling parapet. They peered down. A man was down there. He wasn't a drunk or a local. He was dressed in plain clothes, but he moved with an unmistakable air of calm, professional authority. In one hand, he held a powerful torch, its beam sweeping back and forth in a patient, analytical grid. In the other, he held a clipboard.

"Police," Rahul breathed, the word a puff of pure, freezing ice in the night air.

Chung's hand shot out and clamped onto his forearm, her grip as hard and unyielding as a metal vise. "Stay low," she hissed, her voice barely a whisper.

They pressed themselves flat against the cold concrete, their hearts hammering in a painful, suffocating rhythm against their ribs. They watched as the man moved with a chilling efficiency, his boots crunching on the broken ground with a steady, unhurried rhythm. He stopped at the edge of the crater—*their crater*—and knelt, the movement precise and unhurried.

"Think he knows?" Chung whispered, her voice so faint it was nearly stolen by the wind.

"He's not here for the sightseeing," Rahul whispered back, his throat suddenly tight and dry.

They watched, helpless and frozen, as the man ran a gloved hand through the dirt right where they had been digging. He lifted his fingers into the powerful beam of the torch. Even from this distance, they could see it: the unmistakable, damning glitter of gold dust clinging to the black fabric of his glove. The man stared at it for a long moment, and then a faint, cold smile of discovery touched his lips—a predator that has found the trail. With a slow, deliberate motion, he made a note on his clipboard. The tiny, imagined scratch of his pen felt like a nail being driven into their own coffin. After a final, sweeping look around the desolate landscape, he turned and walked away, his footsteps steady and unhurried, a man who had found exactly what he was looking for.

Chung exhaled slowly—a shuddering, silent breath she hadn't realized she was holding.

"Maybe he's just surveying," she muttered.

Maybe.

Rahul didn't answer immediately.

He stared at the dark crater below.

And the gold dust scattered like crushed galaxies across the rubble.

At the invisible web of greed and violence slowly stitching itself around them.

"Maybe," he said finally.

"But maybe not for long."

The truth hung heavy between them.

They had time.

But not much.

The city's teeth were already closing around them.

The dream was still alive—but the wolves were circling now.

And Mumbai was a city that ate secrets for breakfast.

They returned to the warehouse not with relief, but wrapped in a chilling, shared silence that was more terrifying than any scream. When they slipped through the broken door, Dev and Sujata, who had been sitting in a tense but quiet companionship, looked up. The fragile peace that had settled between them evaporated instantly, replaced by a sudden, electric dread.

Rahul and Chung didn't need to speak. The terror was a physical presence on them—in the stiff, haunted set of Rahul's shoulders and the cold, feral vigilance in Chung's eyes. Sujata's heart seized in a vise of pure, cold panic. *They know,* was her first, wild, and utterly wrong thought. *They somehow know about Vikrant. They know I've brought more trouble to our door.* She instinctively pulled the sleeves of her hoodie further down her arms, a futile attempt to hide bruises no one had even seen yet.

They settled into their broken circle, but the space was no longer a sanctuary. It was a trap, and the walls felt like they were closing in. Dev felt the shift immediately. He had been watching Sujata, noticing the slight, persistent tremor in her hands and the way she jumped at every small sound from the street. He had been about to ask her if she was okay. But now, a new and sharper fear had entered the room, a cold wave radiating from Rahul and Chung. He stayed silent, his protective instincts now split between two separate, invisible fires, his confusion warring with a rising sense of utter dread.

Chung sat with her back pressed against the cold concrete wall, her guitar lying untouched beside her like a fallen soldier. Her eyes, sharp and unblinking, scanned every shadow, every potential entry point, like an animal expecting an ambush. Rahul picked up a stick and began sketching in the thick dust, his movements jerky and agitated. He wasn't drawing logos for a dream anymore. He was drawing maps. Escape routes. Plans that had nothing to do with building a future and everything to do with surviving the next hour.

Suddenly, a distant siren wailed, a lonely, rising cry that sliced through the city's constant hum.

As one, all four of them froze. Their heads snapped up. Their eyes met across the circle. In that single, shared, and utterly terrifying look, the truth was finally passed between them without a single word. They didn't know the specific details of each other's fear—the man with the clipboard, the ghost of an abusive boss—but they all knew the central, damning fact: the world was closing in. The gold had bought them a fleeting, beautiful dream. Now, it was only buying them time, and they all knew, with a certainty that was as cold and hard as the concrete beneath them, that time was running out.

CHAPTER FIFTEEN

KINDLING

Tonight, the air smelled of petrichor, the sweet, earthy scent of the day's surprise shower on the city's hot, dry dust. It was a smell of cleansing, of peace, a fragile truce with the suffocating tension of the past few days. They met at the warehouse not out of habit, but out of a shared, unspoken need. There was no gold to move, no new threat to debate. They came because their own small, lonely rooms had begun to feel like cages again, and this dusty, broken space was the only place in the sprawling, indifferent city where they felt truly seen.

Chung was there first, sitting cross-legged on the dusty concrete, her guitar across her lap. She wasn't playing the angry, distorted riffs she used as armor on the streets. She was plucking a slow, clean, melancholic melody, the notes twisting through the cavernous space like smoke, a sound that acknowledged their shared weariness without surrendering to it. In the faint lantern light, with her hoodie pushed back and her hair messy, she looked almost young, a glimpse of the girl she might have been if the world hadn't forced her to become a warrior.

Rahul arrived next, a clumsy bearer of gifts. In one hand, he carried a precarious, dripping stack of styrofoam cups of cutting chai, and in the other, a plastic bag bulging with hot, greasy vada pavs wrapped in newspaper. "Fuel," he announced gruffly, placing his offerings in the center of their circle like a man unaccustomed to and slightly embarrassed by acts of domestic care. Chung stopped playing and gave him a mock salute before reaching for a cup, a rare, genuine smile touching her lips.

Dev and Sujata arrived a few moments later, walking in together. They didn't touch, but the space between them seemed to hum with a new, quiet, and undeniable energy. Dev's limp was almost gone, a testament to the quiet visit he'd paid to an off-the-books doctor. His posture was straighter, as if a great physical and emotional weight had been lifted from his shoulders. Sujata had shed the defensive armor of her old hoodie. Tonight, she wore a simple, faded yellow kurta that seemed to catch the lantern light and glow, a small, stubborn sun that had refused to set.

Chung saw it immediately. A sly, knowing smirk curved her lips before she looked down and plucked another lazy, suggestive chord on her guitar. Rahul saw it too and grinned quietly into his chai. Some things, they all understood, were too new and fragile to be spoken aloud. They ate in a comfortable, hungry silence, the simple, greasy vada pavs and scalding chai a welcome feast. Outside, the city roared and howled, but inside these battered walls, the world was still. It felt safe.

As the food vanished, the conversation drifted, slow and meandering, the talk of people finally allowing themselves to look past the next twenty-four hours. "I was thinking," Rahul said, sketching on the back of a cigarette carton, "the logo for the courier company should have a wing, but also a lightning bolt. For speed."

Dev, feeling a rush of boldness, looked at Chung. "Maybe one day you could teach me to play guitar?"

Chung gave him a deadpan look. "One vada pav per lesson. No refunds."

Sujata laughed, a soft, tinkling sound that was still strange and wonderful in the empty space. "Only if you agree to be the resident musician for our underground courier and chai empire," she teased.

Slowly, as the night deepened and their laughter faded into a comfortable quiet, Chung stood up, mumbling something about needing a smoke. She wandered toward the entrance, pulling a half-broken bidi from behind her ear. Rahul, after a moment's hesitation, followed her. "I'll just... check the perimeter," he said, the old excuse now sounding flimsy and fond. Their departure was a quiet, unspoken conspiracy, a deliberate, gentle act of leaving the two of them alone. Again.

For a long time, they didn't speak, but the silence was not empty. It was a comfortable, easy quiet, familiar in a way that was both dangerous and inevitable. They sat against opposite pillars, legs stretched out in the dust, the last of the cold chai in its thermos.

"Were you ever married?" Sujata asked, her voice gentle, breaking the quiet without shattering it.

Dev blinked, caught off guard by the personal nature of the question. A soft, self-deprecating laugh escaped him. "God, no," he said, shaking his head. "No one in their right mind would marry a guy who smells like sweat and diesel oil half the time."

She smiled then, a real smile that crinkled the corners of her eyes. "You?" he asked.

Sujata shrugged, her gaze dropping as she picked at a fraying thread on her jeans. "Almost," she said. "Once. A long, long time ago." She didn't elaborate, and he didn't ask. He understood the weight of things left unsaid, of roads not taken and dreams buried too deep to be cleanly excavated.

An unconscious magnetic pull seemed to draw them closer. He shifted. So did she. Their shoulders didn't touch, but the space between them had changed, the air now charged and electric. He scratched the back of his neck awkwardly, his heart starting a low, anxious drumbeat.

"You know," he muttered, the words almost lost in the vastness of the warehouse, "you're scary brave."

Sujata raised an eyebrow, a half-smirk playing on her lips. "Me?"

He nodded, finding a sudden, desperate courage. "You fought through hell for your niece. You stood up to your boss. You've fought this whole damn city." He looked down at his own calloused, battered hands. "I just... survived."

Sujata leaned forward, crossing the invisible line between them. She reached out and, with a gentleness that was almost shocking, tipped his chin up with two fingers, forcing him to meet her gaze. Her eyes were soft, but her voice was steel.

"Surviving *is* fighting, Dev," she said softly. "You didn't break. After everything, you're still here, and you're still good. That's a different kind of brave. Maybe the bravest kind."

The way she said his name, soft and fierce and full of an understanding he had never known, made his chest ache. For a dizzying second, the only thought in his head was the overwhelming, impossible urge to kiss her.

But he didn't. Instead, he let out a shuddering breath and whispered, his voice rough and raw with an emotion he couldn't name, "You make me want to be better."

Sujata's smile returned, small and shy and utterly real. "You already are," she said simply.

And for the first time in his entire life, Dev believed it.

Meanwhile, Outside...

Rahul and Chung leaned against the cool, crumbling brick of the outer wall, the scent of petrichor still heavy in the air. Rahul wasn't smoking this time; he was methodically checking the tension of the drive chain on the borrowed Pulsar by the weak light of his phone.

"You're thinking about the man with the clipboard," Chung said, her voice a low vibration in the dark.

Rahul straightened, his joints popping with a sound like dry twigs. "He didn't look like a scavenger, Chung. He looked like a man who knows exactly what he's looking for." He looked back at the warehouse where the warm glow of the lantern illuminated Dev and Sujata. "We're running out of 'Meanwhile,' aren't we?"

Chung watched the silhouettes inside—two shadows finally finding a moment of peace. Her artist's eye saw the fragility of the scene, a composition that could be shattered by a single siren.

"They're starting to believe the dream is already here," she said, her hand resting on the neck of her guitar case, where the gold was hidden. "That makes them vulnerable. If that inspector comes with backup... if things get messy... you take them and head for the farm shack."

Rahul stopped his work and looked her in the eye, the office-worker slump gone from his shoulders. "We aren't splitting the shares again, Chung. We go together, or we don't go at all."

For the first time, Chung didn't offer a cynical retort. She simply gave a short, sharp nod—a silent contract between the two of them to act as the steel for the two dreamers inside.

Inside the warehouse, Dev and Sujata were discovering something soft and new between them. And out here, under the broken stars, Rahul and Chung had just forged something hard, silent, and unbreakable. In a world that was designed to shatter them, they were learning, piece by piece, how to hold each other together. For tonight, they were safe. For tonight, they were golden. And they had no way of knowing that far away, in the city's dark and hungry heart, the real storm was finally gathering its strength.

CHAPTER SIXTEEN

COLLISION COURSE

Morning in Mumbai never arrived politely. It didn't nudge the city awake with gentle golden beams; it assaulted it. The first attack was sound: the violent, metallic screech of the 4:15 a.m. local train, a sound that ripped through the thin fabric of the night. It was followed by a rising, percussive cacophony that kicked doors open, screamed through tin roofs with the first roar of a thousand awakening engines, and rattled glass with the clatter of steel shutters being raised in a single, city-wide wave. It was a thief that stole the quiet hours, dragging reluctant, exhausted people from whatever fragile dreams they had dared to have, pulling them back into the harsh, unforgiving light of another day of survival. And for the four souls who had touched a piece of a fallen star, who had for a few precious nights allowed themselves to dream, this particular morning was dragging reality back with a special kind of vengeance. It was a reality that was sharper, heavier, and far more dangerous than anything they had known before.

The First Tremors

Rahul was ripped from a shallow, dreamless sleep by the violent screech of metal on asphalt directly below his window. The sound bypassed his conscious mind entirely and hit him like a physical blow. *Raid. They're here. They found me.* The thought was a bolt of pure, unreasoning panic. His heart seized in his chest as he scrambled from his thin mattress, his limbs clumsy with sleep and terror. He stumbled to the window, his breath held tight, fully expecting to see the flashing lights of a police jeep.

Instead, he saw a mundane, pathetic scene of city life. A scooter lay on its side, its front wheel bent at a sickening, unnatural angle. Two men, their faces contorted with rage, were shouting at each other, their angry voices echoing in the narrow, pre-dawn stillness. It wasn't a raid. It was just another Mumbai morning.

Rahul slumped against the wall, his forehead slick with a cold sweat, his legs suddenly weak with a relief that was almost as painful as the fear had been. But the terror didn't recede. It lingered, a new and unwelcome tenant in his body. He pressed a hand to his chest, trying to calm the frantic, wild hammering of his heart. This was his new life, he realized. A life of phantom sirens and heart-stopping fear at every loud noise. He was discovering the terrible, cruel irony of hope: for all the years he had wanted to die, he had never truly been afraid. Now that he finally had something to live for, he had everything to lose.

Across the city, Sujata was experiencing the first, sweet, intoxicating taste of that hope. She signed the hospital's release forms with a hand that was, for the first time in memory, perfectly steady. The act of paying for Anaya's next round of tests in advance, with cash, without begging or borrowing, was a small, powerful miracle that made her feel almost dizzy with relief. Anaya, vibrant with a new, healthy energy, skipped beside her, chattering excitedly about a movie she wanted to see. Sujata smiled, a genuine, unforced expression that felt like a sunrise on her own face. *A real birthday this year,* she thought, the idea a sudden, brilliant bloom in her mind. *With a real cake. And balloons. And all her friends.*

As they waited for the elevator, a flicker of movement down the long, sterile hall caught her eye. A man, sitting on a bench near the pharmacy. She glanced away, then her gaze was pulled back. Something was wrong. He was wearing dark sunglasses indoors, a jarring affectation in the dim hospital light. He was pretending to scroll through his phone, but his thumb wasn't moving. And his posture... it wasn't the relaxed slump of someone waiting. It was a tense, coiled stillness. His head was angled just slightly, almost imperceptibly, in her direction.

A cold dread began to wash over her, chilling the warm hope in her veins. *Am I being paranoid?* But the feeling was too specific, too familiar. It was the feeling of being prey. Her mind raced. *Is it Vikrant? Did he follow me here? Or did he send someone?* The uncertainty was almost worse than the confirmation.

The elevator pinged its arrival. Without a second thought, Sujata's body moved with a primal, protective instinct. She scooped Anaya into her arms, pulling the little girl's face into her shoulder, shielding her from the unseen gaze down the hall. "We're taking the stairs, baby," she muttered, her voice a tight, breathless whisper as she turned and hurried in the opposite direction, her heart now a frantic, terrified drum against Anaya's back.

Dev, meanwhile, felt like a king. The roar of his own engine was a song of pure liberation. He weaved the battered Honda through the morning traffic, not as a victim, but as a participant. For the first time, the city's chaos wasn't a force to be endured; it was a dance, and he was finally a part of it. A gap opened between a bus and an auto-rickshaw, and he shot through it with a surge of adrenaline and a triumphant grin. He was fast. He was free. He was, for a few glorious moments, completely untouchable.

Then he glanced at his one good side mirror. A crack ran through the glass like a spider's web, fracturing the world behind him. In the largest piece of the mirror, he saw a persistent black shape. A Pulsar motorcycle. Two riders. They were hanging back, a little too far to be aggressive, a little too close to be casual. He dismissed it. Just more traffic.

He took a sharp left to a bypass road. As he straightened out, he checked the mirror again. The black Pulsar was still there, making the same turn, settling in behind him once more. A cold knot began to tighten in his stomach. *Coincidence.* He decided to test it. He deliberately eased off the throttle, letting his speed drop. The roar of the engine softened, and the city's noise rushed back in. He watched the mirror. The Pulsar slowed down too, its distance from him remaining exactly, precisely the same.

It was not a coincidence.

The blood ran cold in his veins. His mouth went instantly dry, the exhilarating taste of freedom replaced by the familiar, bitter taste of fear. With a surge of pure panic, he gunned the engine. The joyful dance became a frantic, desperate flight. He pulled a series of reckless maneuvers, swerving between cars, cutting off a rickshaw, and earning a chorus of angry horns that he barely heard. He just needed to get away. After two more chaotic turns, he risked another glance. They were gone. He pulled over to the side of the road, his hands trembling on the handlebars. Were they really gone? Or had they just proven their point? The song of liberation was over. He was no longer a king. He was just prey who had been given a head start.

Chung, as always, sought refuge in becoming invisible. She found a spot on the edge of the Bandra promenade, her open guitar case at her feet, and began to strum. The music she played was deliberately forgettable—a series of half-finished, meandering chords that were designed to blend seamlessly with the sounds of the crashing waves and the distant roar of traffic. It was the perfect camouflage, turning her into just another piece of the city's scenery. But while her fingers moved with a practiced, lazy ease, her eyes were sharp, cold, and constantly in motion.

She wasn't watching the laughing couples or the breathless joggers. She was watching for the watchers. Her artist's eye, trained to see details others missed, was now a finely tuned threat-detection system. She scanned for the men who walked with the heavy, purposeful gait of off-duty cops. She looked for the tell-tale bulge of a jacket that didn't hang quite right. She noted the unmarked car that passed by the same spot twice. Her gaze lingered on anyone whose stillness was too predatory, whose own eyes were also scanning, hunting.

And today, the rhythm of the city felt wrong. The background hum had a new, sharper undertone, a discordant note in a familiar song. It was in the way a group of teenagers suddenly quieted their laughter, in the subtle, almost imperceptible tensing of the street vendor's shoulders down the way. It was a collective, subconscious holding of the breath. It was the subtle, chilling shift in the air that a forest animal senses just moments before the hunter reveals himself. She didn't know where the threat was coming from, but she knew, with a certainty that was as cold and hard as the stone beneath her, that it was coming.

The Hunters Mobilize

In a humid, subterranean parking garage that smelled of damp concrete and exhaust, Vikrant slammed the trunk of his car shut. The sound was a flat, violent boom that echoed in the enclosed space. Inside the trunk, nestled in a metal case, were the tools of his reclamation: a heavy, unregistered revolver, a Maglite flashlight sturdy enough to break bone, and a packet of thick plastic zip ties. He slid into the driver's seat, the car's interior reeking of stale cigarette smoke and his own simmering fury. His thoughts were a vicious, looping reel of humiliation. It wasn't just about Sujata anymore. It was about the boy who had dared to protect her, about the entire universe that had conspired to make him a laughingstock. He wasn't just hunting her; he was hunting all of them. He drove up the ramp and out into the chaotic morning traffic, his hands gripping the steering wheel so tightly his knuckles were white, his mind already savoring the image of their collective terror.

At that exact same moment, across the city, Inspector D'Souza stood in the bland, sterile, and aggressively air-conditioned lobby of a corporate building in Andheri East. He wasn't in uniform, but his quiet authority was a tangible, suffocating force in the room. He tapped his government ID rhythmically against his palm, his gaze fixed on the terrified young receptionist, a predator enjoying the fear of his prey.

"Rahul Sharma," he repeated, his voice patient, calm, and utterly unyielding.

"Y-yes, sir," the young woman stammered, a bead of sweat trickling down her temple. "He works here. In accounts. But he's been... out of the office a lot. Fieldwork," he says.

D'Souza gave a slow, thoughtful nod, his mind a cold, efficient machine connecting the dots. He had spent the morning in the city's grimy underbelly, visiting the back-alley jewelers and scrap dealers from his informant list. He'd heard the same disjointed whispers at each stop: a nervous, desperate-looking group selling small, strange batches of "dirty gold." The descriptions were consistent: a tired, middle-aged office worker. An injured young man. Two women. It was a picture slowly coming into focus. And now, thanks to a quiet threat to a low-level clerk, he had a name. The net, which had been cast wide, was now closing. And Inspector D'Souza was a very, very patient fisherman.

The Collision

That night, the warehouse was no longer a sanctuary; it was a cage, and the walls were closing in. The air was thick with the sour, metallic smell of their collective, rising fear.

"They're onto us," Sujata said, the words blunt and hard, her voice trembling as she told them about the man in sunglasses at the hospital.

As she finished, Dev nodded grimly. "Two men on a black Pulsar tailed me this morning," he added, his voice low. "They were professionals."

Chung let out a string of soft, vicious curses in a language the others didn't understand. "Cops?"

"Or worse," Rahul said, running a hand through his hair, his face pale. "Every street-level thug in this city knows something fell. We were just the first ones to get there."

"We have to move the gold," Chung said, her voice a sharp, urgent command. "We have to run tonight."

"Where?" Sujata cried, her voice cracking with the sheer, hopeless terror of the question. "There's nowhere to go!"

"My uncle," Dev said, the idea coming to him in a sudden, desperate rush. "He has an old, abandoned farm shack. An hour outside the city, near Panvel."

"Can you trust him?" Rahul asked, his voice sharp with doubt.

Dev gave a bitter, humorless smile. "He drinks so much he barely remembers his own name. He won't even know we're there."

"It's a huge risk," Rahul countered. "We'd be exposed on the open road."

"Staying here is a death sentence!" Chung shot back.

They looked at each other, their faces pale and haunted in the lantern light. It was a terrible, desperate, and deeply flawed plan. It was the only plan they had. They made a fatal, tragic miscalculation. They would gather their things, prepare, and leave under the cover of the next night. But fate does not wait for plans.

As Sujata and Dev were leaving later, rounding the corner into a familiar, dark alley, a figure detached itself from the shadows. Vikrant. His eyes were wild and bloodshot, and the stench of cheap whiskey rolled off him in waves.

"Going somewhere, whore?" he hissed, his hand clamping down on Sujata's arm like a vise. "You owe me." He slammed her hard against the brick wall, the impact knocking the air from her lungs. "I'll sell that sick little niece of yours to a brothel! You hear me?"

Before Sujata could even find the breath to scream, a roar of pure, animal fury erupted from behind them. Dev. He hadn't just been walking with her; he had been watching her, guarding her. He moved not like a victim, but like a storm. In his hand was the heavy, greasy motorcycle chain he'd taken from his old bike, its links wrapped tight around his knuckles. He swung it in a vicious, whistling arc that cracked hard against Vikrant's shoulder. Vikrant howled in pain, stumbling back. Dev didn't hesitate. He charged, no longer the boy who got beaten in an alley, but the man who was ending the fight. He fought with the raw, brutal desperation of a man who has finally found something more important to defend than himself. Vikrant, bleeding, his bravado shattered by the sheer ferocity of the attack, scrambled to his feet and fled into the labyrinth of the night, screaming threats and curses.

Dev stood panting, the heavy chain dropping from his hand with a clatter. He turned to Sujata, his chest heaving, and pulled her into a fierce, protective embrace. "I've got you," he whispered into her hair, a raw, unbreakable promise.

And far across the city, in a quiet, sterile, brightly lit office, Inspector D'Souza picked up his pen. He looked down at the freshly printed arrest warrants for one Rahul Sharma and three as-yet-unidentified associates, for questioning in the matter of an unregistered celestial impact. He signed his name with a neat, final flourish. Tomorrow morning, at dawn, he would bring them in. The sky, it seemed, was about to fall on them all over again.

CHAPTER SEVENTEEN

The Night We Burned

The warehouse was no longer a sanctuary; it was a tomb waiting for bodies. The attack on Sujata had shattered their last illusion of time.

"Tomorrow is a fantasy," Chung said, her voice a flat, cold blade that sliced through their panicked silence. "That man, Vikrant, he's either going to the police or he's coming back with friends. We run. Tonight. Now."

The words landed with the force of a final judgment. The air was instantly thick with the silent, frantic energy of preparation. Rahul began to pace in tight, aggressive circles, his mind a frantic, flashing map of the city's arteries and veins, searching for an escape route, a path without a blockade. Every distant shout and every backfiring engine from the city outside was now the sound of approaching sirens.

Chung, moving with a tense, vibrating energy, became the center of their new reality. "Phones," she commanded. One by one, they handed them over. Without a word of explanation, she took each cheap plastic phone, snapped it in half over her knee with a sharp crack, pried out the tiny

SIM card, and crushed it to dust under the heel of her boot. It was a brutal, final act of erasure. They were no longer just hiding; they were becoming ghosts.

Dev stood by the entrance, a silent, grim sentinel. The raw, swollen skin on his knuckles was a testament to the fight, and the throbbing pain was a grounding, focusing force. The terror of the past few days had burned away the last of the victim in him. He was no longer just a survivor; he was a guard dog, every muscle coiled, his gaze fixed on the darkness outside, ready to meet the first sign of danger with a violence that was new and terrifying to him.

Sujata stood near the small pile of their remaining gold, the cloth bundles looking small and pathetic in the vast, dark room. She clutched her backpack strap, her face pale, her fear a cold, hard knot in her stomach. It was a fear not for herself, but for the life she had just started to imagine for Anaya, a life that was now about to be swallowed by the night.

"They'll come for us," she whispered, the words a confirmation of Chung's hard truth.

"Let them," Dev said, his voice a low growl, not turning from the door. "We stick to the plan. Uncle's farm. We stash the gold, and we disappear."

Sujata's voice was a thin, terrified thread in the darkness. "What if they find us on the road?"

Dev met her gaze, and in his hard, determined eyes, she saw not confidence, but a grim, unbreakable resolve. "Then we run faster," he said, the words a simple, brutal promise.

"Two bikes," Chung stated, her voice cutting through their fear, taking command. "Two teams. We leave five minutes apart. Dev and Sujata first." It was a smart plan. It was a terrifying gamble. With a shared, grim nod, they moved.

While Dev checked every bolt on his battered bike, his hands surprisingly steady, Rahul secured the gold parcels, his fingers pulling the knots so tight his knuckles were white. "Ready?" Rahul finally asked, his voice hoarse. They all nodded. There was no other choice.

Dev kicked his bike to life; the engine's sputtering cough was a single, violent gunshot in the silence. Sujata swung on behind him, her arms locking around his waist in a desperate, grounding grip. They exchanged a single, hard look with Rahul and Chung, a look of soldiers going over the top of a trench. Then, with a sharp twist of the throttle, they plunged out of the warehouse's darkness and into the hostile, waiting city.

As they fled, the net was already tightening. In Rahul's now-empty apartment, Inspector D'Souza moved with a calm, predatory grace. The cheap lock had been an insult. The room itself was a story of frantic, clumsy escape—an open, empty drawer, a mattress askew, and the faint indentation on the bed where a heavy bag had recently sat. *They're running,* he thought, a cold, professional smile touching his lips. He pulled out his radio. "All units," he said, his voice calm and precise, like a surgeon making an incision. "Suspects are mobile. Two motorcycles, four individuals. Likely heading out of the city via the Eastern Express Highway. Establish a perimeter. I want every exit point covered. Now." In the far distance, the first sirens began their mournful, rising howl.

Back at the warehouse, Rahul and Chung waited in an agony of silence, counting the seconds. Every passing headlight was a potential police car, every distant shout a closing hunter. The five minutes felt like five years. Finally, it was time. Rahul mounted their borrowed Pulsar, its engine catching with a smoother, more powerful roar.

Chung climbed on behind, her arms wrapping around his chest with a surprising, steely strength. With another twist of an engine, they too were gone, two more ghosts swallowed by the Mumbai night.

At that exact moment, Vikrant was prowling the alleys near Sujata's chawl like a caged, rabid animal. He saw her empty window, the cheap curtains fluttering in the breeze like a taunt. He punched the brick wall in a fit of impotent rage, the pain in his knuckles a satisfying echo of the fury in his gut. Then he heard it: the distinct, angry roar of two motorcycles peeling out onto the main road not far away. His head snapped up. He saw their taillights, two pairs of fleeing red eyes, disappearing into the traffic. It was them. He knew it with a certainty that was as hot and vicious as his own blood. With a snarl, he scrambled for his own bike, his mind consumed by a single, burning thought: *I will make them pay.*

The city dissolved into a smear of bleeding neon, dust, and diesel smoke. The engines screamed like wounded animals, their high-pitched wail a constant soundtrack to the frantic, hammering fists of their own hearts. The world tilted and spun beneath them—an unstable, angry, and terrifyingly alive obstacle course.

Dev gritted his teeth, every muscle in his body wound into a tight, screaming coil as he gunned the battered Honda. The gold bundle, tucked inside his jacket, thudded against his bruised ribs with every bone-jarring bounce—a second, heavy, and incriminating heartbeat. Sujata clung to him, a fierce, desperate anchor in the chaos. Her fingers trembled, not with fear anymore, but with a raw, defiant refusal—a refusal to let go, a refusal to die forgotten in some gutter, and a refusal to lose him.

Ahead, the old Pulsar bucked and rattled under the strain as Rahul pushed it to its limit, his hands aching, his knuckles white. Chung was pressed tight against his back, her arms locked around him like steel cables. In his side mirror, the world was a horror show of flashing red and blue. The police. Too close. Gaining.

"Twist left! Now!" Chung's sharp voice barked from the bike beside him, a command cutting through the roar of the engines. "No main roads!"

Rahul responded instantly, wrenching his bike into a narrow side alley that was little more than a crack between two buildings. Trash cans toppled in their wake, the clatter swallowed by the scream of their engines. Dev followed, the Honda's handlebars scraping hard against a brick wall, sending a shower of sparks into the darkness. The air was suddenly thick with the suffocating stench of rotting garbage. Sweat stung Dev's eyes, and every shallow, burning breath was a battle. He didn't dare slow down.

He glanced in his mirror again. The police cars were too wide for the alley and were forced to go around. But Vikrant, on his nimbler bike and fueled by pure, obsessive rage, had followed them in. He was closing the distance.

Up ahead, the frantic, rhythmic clang of a railway crossing bell began to sound—a death knell in the night. The rusted barrier arm, with a shudder of old machinery, started its slow descent.

"We're not going to make it!" Rahul yelled over the wind, his voice thin with panic.

"We have to!" Dev roared back, a sound of pure, desperate will. He twisted the throttle as far as it would go. The engine screamed a high, protesting wail. Sujata clung to him, her face buried in his back, her arms a steel band around his waist, a silent, trusting anchor in the chaos.

He aimed for the gap. They hit the tracks at full speed. The bike bucked violently, a bone-jarring impact that sent a shockwave of pain through his already battered body and nearly threw them both. For a horrifying, weightless half-second, they were airborne. They landed on the other side with a brutal, teeth-rattling crash, the back tire clearing the second track just as the barrier slammed down behind them with a deafening, final clang.

A moment later, from the other side, came the sickening crunch of metal on metal. Vikrant had tried to follow, but as the barrier dropped, his front tire caught the edge of the rising track bed. The bike fishtailed violently, sliding out from under him in a spray of sparks and tortured metal. He was thrown hard onto the gravel, his shoulder taking the brunt of the slide before his bike tumbled into a chaotic heap near the signal post.

They had a few seconds' lead. But the momentary victory was hollow. The sirens were louder now, closer, no longer behind them but on all sides, a tightening net of sound. The city was no longer a place to live; it was a hunting ground, and they were the prey.

"Almost there! Hold on!" Dev shouted over his shoulder as he wrenched the bike into a narrow, unlit service alley, the handlebars scraping against brick in a shower of sparks. And then the ground simply vanished. The front tire plunged into a massive, unseen pothole with a sickening, frame-shattering crunch. The handlebars were torn from Dev's hands with brutal, bone-breaking force. The world became a sickening, sideways blur of motion and sound.

Sujata's scream was cut short as they were thrown, two ragdolls, into the darkness.

Dev hit the asphalt hard, the impact a sickening crack that echoed from his ribs as the air was driven from his lungs in a pained whoosh. He tumbled, a chaotic mess of flailing limbs, his head finally slamming against a concrete pole with a dull, wet, final thud. Sujata skidded across the rough, gravelly ground, the asphalt shredding the skin from her palms and knee in a single, searing, white-hot flash of pain that momentarily blotted out the world.

She forced herself up, her vision a swimming, nauseating blur. "Dev!" she gasped, her voice a raw croak as she scrambled toward his crumpled, unmoving form. "Dev, please," she sobbed, crawling the last few feet, her bleeding hands leaving streaks on the wet ground. She grabbed his jacket. "Get up. Please, get up." Blood was trickling from a gash on his temple, dark and terrifying.

But his eyes fluttered open, a flicker of stubborn, pained light in their depths. He groaned, pushing himself up with agonizing slowness. "I'm... okay," he rasped, a blatant lie that was also the bravest thing she had ever heard.

Just then, the roar of the second bike filled the alley as Rahul and Chung skidded to a halt beside them. Rahul cursed, his face a mask of pure horror at the wreckage. Chung was already off the bike before it had fully stopped, her eyes not on them but scanning the ground. As Sujata skidded across the rough ground, her backpack caught on a jagged metal grate, the fabric ripping with a violent screech. Dozens of the heavy, glittering pellets cascaded out, disappearing into the black, churning water of the storm drain with a series of tiny, mocking splashes. Chung lunged for the scattered trail, her fingers clawing at the oily mud, but a sweep of a police flashlight from the end of the alley forced her back. She snatched up the remaining, half-empty bundle, the weight in her hand sickeningly light. "Leave it!" Rahul hissed, grabbing her arm. "The sirens are right on us!"

"No more bikes," Rahul said grimly, hauling Dev to his feet, Dev leaning heavily on him. "We run."

Ahead, the black, gaping mouth of a massive, half-collapsed storm drain yawned open. "In there!" Rahul yelled.

Chung dove in first without hesitation, disappearing into the foul darkness. Sujata and Rahul half-carried the groaning, stumbling Dev after her, plunging into the suffocating stench of mold and rat droppings. Their frantic, splashing footsteps were a horrifying echo in the narrow pipe, punctuated by the sudden, angry shouts from the alley behind them. Sharp, cutting beams from powerful flashlights sliced through the entrance, too close.

They stumbled deeper into the labyrinth, slipping and sliding on the slick, uneven floor. At a fork, Chung, running on pure, animal instinct, chose a path, and they followed, the sounds of their pursuers finally, blessedly, beginning to fade. They ran until their lungs burned, until they were no longer four people but a single, four-part entity of pain and desperation, held together by sheer, ragged will.

Finally, the tunnel opened into a small, overgrown, and trash-filled hollow beneath an abandoned overpass. They collapsed in the shadows, a tangled, bleeding, and gasping heap. For a long time, the only sound was their own ragged, desperate breathing.

Dev sagged against a concrete pillar, his face a pale, grey mask slick with blood, but he managed a weak, crooked smile. He was alive. Sujata knelt before him, tears of relief and fury streaming down her face, mixing with the grime.

"You're a terrible liar," she choked out. He chuckled, a terrible, rattling sound from his bruised ribs. "Learned from the best."

Nearby, Rahul slumped to the ground, trying futilely to wipe the blood from his own scraped knuckles. Chung sat beside him, cradling the mud-stained gold bundle like a wounded, priceless child. She looked into the half-empty bag, her fingers tracing the jagged tear where the rest of their future had spilled into the gutter. She met Rahul's eyes in the dark, a silent, hollow apology passing between them. They were alive, but the weight of what they had lost felt heavier than the metal they had kept. They were broken. They were bleeding. But they were alive. And they were together. For now, that was more than enough.

CHAPTER EIGHTEEN

RISE OR FALL

The city of Mumbai did not forgive. It was a sprawling, sleepless organism with a million eyes and an infinite memory, a place of debts recorded on faded ledgers and slights remembered for generations in the glint of a stranger's eye. It never slept, and it never, ever forgot a weakness. But sometimes, if a story was small enough, if the lives lived were quiet enough, if the people in it were clever enough, desperate enough, and impossibly, breathtakingly lucky, the city did something far more merciful than forgiving. It forgot.

It wasn't an act of kindness. It was a momentary lapse in the beast's all-seeing, crushing attention, a single dropped stitch in its vast, chaotic tapestry. And in a city that remembered everything, that small, temporary blindness was enough. It was enough to slip through the deep cracks in its concrete skin, enough to catch a single, ragged, and precious breath in the suffocating air, and enough to begin the impossible, audacious work of rebuilding a life that fate, and the city, had tried so ruthlessly to drown.

Two days after they had crawled out of the storm drain, they huddled like wounded animals in the back room of an abandoned tea shop on the far, forgotten outskirts of the city. The air was thick with the cloying, sweet smell of old, spilled tea that had fermented into a scent of pure decay. A steady drip from a leak in the roof plopped into a stagnant puddle in the corner, a maddeningly rhythmic clock counting out their borrowed time. Their collective gaze was fixed on the rickety table in the center of the room. On it sat three battered cloth bundles, a pathetic-looking treasure that was a grim testament to everything they had gained and nearly lost. A significant portion of the gold—their future—was gone, lost somewhere in the filthy gutters of the city. What remained was enough, but only just.

They were a collection of fresh, angry wounds. Dev sat slumped against the wall, a raw, ugly line of black stitches bisecting his eyebrow, a permanent reminder of his impact with the pole. Sujata sat stiffly in a cracked plastic chair, her heavily bandaged knee propped up. Rahul took every breath in a shallow, painful hiss, the heavy tape around his ribs a constant, sharp reminder of the crash. And Chung's knuckles, from a moment of pure, violent frustration two nights ago, were raw and scabbed.

It was Rahul who broke the heavy silence, his voice a low, grim rasp. "We need a new plan."

Dev looked up; his eyes, shadowed by the new scar, were hard as stone. "No more running," he said, the words a low, guttural growl.

"No more hiding," Chung added, her voice flat, cold, and utterly devoid of fear.

Sujata's hands, still tender and scraped, tightened into fists in her lap. "No more being scared," she finished, her voice quiet but vibrating with a new, unyielding, and dangerous strength.

They looked at each other then, and in that shared, hard-eyed glance, a new pact was forged. The frantic, desperate fear was gone, burned away in the fire of the chase. In its place was something harder, colder, and far more lethal: resolve. They would stop reacting to the city's attacks. They would attack back. Their new plan was no longer about escape; it was about building a fortress. They would sell what was left of the gold, piece by painful, careful piece, and use every rupee to become legitimate, to build businesses, and to become so visible that they would finally disappear into the city's normal, everyday hum. But before they could build their future, they had to systematically hunt down and bury the ghosts of their past.

Closing Vikrant's Chapter

They found Vikrant exactly where his informant said he would be: in a foul-smelling dive bar near Kurla station, a place where old men sat hunched over their glasses in the nicotine-stained gloom, waiting to die. He was at the far end of the bar, a ghost of his former self, staring into a glass of cheap rum. His once-expensive watch was gone, replaced by a pale strip of skin on his wrist. His left arm was bound in a stiff, grimy sling, and the side of his face was a mottled map of yellow and deep purple bruising. A thick bridge of surgical tape held his broken nose in place, and a dark, jagged line of scabs traced the road rash along his jawline.

When Sujata pushed through the swinging door, letting in a slice of the noisy, chaotic street, his head jerked up. Recognition flared in his eyes, and for a moment, his old, greasy smirk returned, an automatic reflex of cruelty. The smirk died the instant Dev limped in behind her. The raw, black stitches bisecting Dev's eyebrow were a clear, brutal reminder of their last encounter, a silent promise of violence.

Sujata walked toward him, her steps even and sure, a queen walking into a conquered territory. She did not waver. She stopped directly in front of him and, with a calm, deliberate motion, placed a small USB drive on the sticky bar counter. It made a soft, sharp click against the glass, a sound that was louder than a gunshot in the quiet, dead air of the bar.

"You will not come near me, or my family, ever again," she said. Her voice was level, cold, and completely devoid of the fear he was used to hearing from her.

He opened his mouth, the sneer returning. "And what are you going to do? Cry to your new boyfriend?" he taunted, nodding toward Dev. "Or did that little phone call I gave you the other night not rattle your cage enough? I wanted to see how long it would take for you rats to start scurrying. Maybe you'll sell him off next to pay for that sick little brat of yours—' The words were meant to break her, but Sujata didn't even flinch. She leaned in, her eyes as hard and cold as stone, the insult turning to ash in the face of her resolve. "If you do," she continued, her voice dropping to a low, dangerous whisper, "you won't just lose what's left of your miserable job. You will lose your freedom." She tapped the USB drive with one long, deliberate finger. "On this is everything. Every chat. Every hidden camera video. Every illegal bank transfer. Not just with me. With all the other girls. Two copies are with two different lawyers. A third is in a sealed envelope, ready to be sent to the cybercrime division."

The last of the color drained from Vikrant's face. He looked from her cold eyes to the small, plastic object on the counter.

"You are one anonymous phone call away from being a national headline," she whispered, her voice a blade in the quiet bar. "One whisper away from becoming the most famous pervert in Mumbai."

From behind her, Dev, who had been standing silent and menacing, shifted his weight. The simple sound of his shoe scraping the dirty floor made Vikrant flinch. The last of his pathetic arrogance crumbled, replaced by the raw, wide-eyed terror of a cornered rat.

"You are nothing now," Sujata said, her voice final. "And you will say nothing."

She turned and walked out without looking back. Dev followed, pausing just long enough to casually backhand Vikrant's glass. Cheap rum spilled across the counter, soaking the USB drive in a final, symbolic act of contempt. As they stepped out into the humid, indifferent night, Vikrant did not shout. He did not curse. He did not even move. He just sat there, staring at the small, wet piece of plastic that now held the leash to his entire miserable life.

Dealing with D'Souza

Chung and Rahul took on the more dangerous side of the battlefield. Inspector D'Souza wasn't a street thug; he was a creature of the system, a man who hid his crimes behind a badge. He couldn't be beaten with fists, and he couldn't be easily bought. But men like him, men who built their power on a carefully constructed illusion of respectability, had one fatal weakness: they were terrified of being exposed.

They spent a frantic forty-eight hours in the city's grimy underbelly. Rahul dusted off old, forgotten contacts from his sales days, his voice a low, urgent murmur in smoky backrooms as he traded favors for the names of clerks D'Souza had shaken down. Chung, with a cold, deadpan precision that was utterly terrifying, slipped bribes to the right people, returning with grainy, long-lens photos of the inspector taking thick envelopes of cash from illegal pawn brokers. It wasn't enough to put him in jail. But it was more than enough to end his career in a blaze of public humiliation.

They met him in a grimy Irani café near CST station, a place where time seemed to have stopped in 1978. The ancient ceiling fans did little more than stir the thick, hot air, which smelled of old smoke, baking bread, and a century of secrets. D'Souza arrived radiating an aura of bored, condescending authority. He sat across from them at the small, stained marble table, a small, smug smile playing on his lips as he sipped his watery chai. He saw them as exactly what they were: a broken-down office worker and a street kid. Rats to be crushed at his leisure.

Rahul's heart was a frantic drum against his ribs, but he forced his hands to be steady as he slid a thick manila envelope across the table. It came to a stop directly in front of D'Souza's cup. Chung, who had been sipping her own chai in a pointed, unnerving silence, finally spoke.

"You will forget about us," she said, her voice soft but carrying the dangerous, unyielding weight of a final command. "You will forget the textile grounds. You will forget the sky ever fell here."

D'Souza's smile tightened into a sneer. With a look of mild, theatrical irritation, he flipped open the envelope. He glanced at the first photo and let out a short, dismissive laugh. 'Is this a joke? I could have you arrested for extortion.' He tossed the photo onto the table, but his eyes betrayed a flicker of something that wasn't amusement. Rahul's heart hammered against his ribs, but Chung didn't move. "Keep reading, Inspector," she said, her voice dangerously calm. "And before you think about having us arrested for extortion, know that a digital copy of every page in that envelope is sitting in a locked queue with a lawyer in South Mumbai. If we don't check in by midnight, those files—and your career—go live to the press. You aren't just looking at a bribe, Inspector. You're looking at your own cage." D'Souza's arrogance began to dissolve as he slid out the next item: a bank statement that should have been buried forever. This time, the color drained from his face. His hands, which had been so steady, began to tremble, just slightly. He looked up, and in the bruised but steady gaze of Rahul and the cold, unblinking eyes of Chung, he saw not rats, but two people who had already been to the bottom and had absolutely nothing left to fear from a man like him.

He carefully, almost tenderly, slid the papers back into the envelope. He had lost. He knew it. With a single, sharp, and utterly defeated nod, a gesture of complete and total surrender, he stood up and walked out of the café without another word, without looking back. The threats were neutralized. The past was severed. And the future, for the first time, was a blank, open, and beckoning road.

New Dreams Taking Root

In the weeks that followed, four small, stubborn seeds of hope began to sprout in the city's unforgiving concrete. In a tiny, rented garage in Andheri that perpetually smelled of petrol and ambition, **Starfall Couriers** was born. It was a chaotic symphony of constantly ringing phones, of young delivery boys shouting jokes and insults in three different languages, and the constant, angry roar of second-hand bikes coming and going. At the center of it all was Rahul, no longer a stooped, defeated man, but a whirlwind of frantic, joyous energy, a general commanding a small, loyal army.

His first and best hire, Dev, moved with a newfound, easy confidence, his limp now just a ghost that appeared on rainy days. He was the logistics manager, the head rider, and the street diplomat, treating every parcel with the fierce, protective focus of a man who knew what it felt like to have everything taken from him.

Across town, the faded yellow door of **Scarlet Café** opened for business. It was a tiny slip of a place, with mismatched chairs and a collection of cracked but clean mugs, but the air was always thick with the comforting, holy smell of strong, sweet chai and fresh vada pav. At first, people came for the cheap food, but they stayed for the warmth. They stayed to watch a healthy, vibrant Anaya doing her homework at a corner table, her easy, bubbling laughter the truest testament to the café's real purpose.

And in a forgotten, dusty storeroom in Mahim, the dissonant, beautiful, and unapologetically loud noise of **The Dreamer's Den** came to life. Chung had filled the space with donated, beat-up guitars and broken amps that buzzed with a life of their own, creating a free music school for the street kids no one else saw. She was a reluctant, impatient, and often terrifyingly blunt teacher, but she taught them more than chords; she taught them, with every angry, distorted riff, that their noise mattered.

Sometimes, late at night, after the last delivery was made and the last cup of chai was washed, the four of them would still meet on a quiet rooftop, a new, secret sanctuary. They would pass around a thermos of Sujata's chai and look out at the glittering, indifferent city that had tried, and failed, to crush them. They didn't talk about gold or fear anymore. They talked about bad clients, leaky faucets, and the absurd, beautiful, and exhausting business of being alive. They were no longer running. They were building.

And they were doing it together.

CHAPTER NINETEEN

THE STARS WE BURIED

Mumbai gleamed under a bruised dusk sky, but it was not the cold, arrogant glitter of the billionaire towers that clawed at the clouds, nor the frantic, hungry pulse of the neon malls. This was a different light. It was the stubborn, lonely glow of a single streetlight clinging to a cracked sidewalk, its yellow light making a halo in the humid air. It was the battered, buzzing neon of a late-night tea stall, a beacon for the city's tired and sleepless. It was the low, hopeful hum of a thousand rickshaw meters, each one ticking another rupee, another dream, into existence. This was the true heartbeat of a city that didn't promise survival but never, ever, let it die completely.

It had been three months. Three months since that same sky had cracked open and bled fire. Three months since four sets of broken, bleeding hands had clawed a desperate, impossible dream from the scorched and broken earth. Three months since four strangers, united only by their shared proximity to the abyss, had stopped simply surviving the city's brutal gravity and had begun the slow, painful, and glorious process of becoming. The first year had been a war of centimeters. There were months when Rahul and Dev shared a single, sputtering bike, alternating shifts until their eyes were red with exhaustion. There were mornings when Sujata served tea from a dented thermos on a street corner, her café nothing more than a patch of shade and a stubborn refusal to move. They had bled for the legitimacy they now wore so easily.

Vindication

About a month after their escape, Rahul was sitting in the cramped, chaotic office of Starfall Couriers, sipping a cup of scalding chai and idly scrolling through a local news app on his phone. He was half-listening to the good-natured arguments of his drivers in the next room when a small, buried headline caught his eye: Geological Survey Officer Resigns Amid Internal Probe. His heart gave a single, hard thud. He tapped the link. The article was short, bland, and full of bureaucratic jargon. It cited "personal reasons" for Inspector D'Souza's abrupt departure and made a vague, unsubstantiated mention of "procedural misconduct. " Rahul read it twice, then a third time. A slow, deeply satisfied smile spread across his face. It wasn't a triumphant, front-page exposé. It was a quiet, bloodless, bureaucratic execution, a stain scrubbed clean in the back rooms of power. No one else in the city would ever know or care. It was the perfect, anonymous, and utterly powerless end for a man who had tried to steal their future. Chung found her own, quieter vindication in the digital archives of a local newspaper. For weeks, she had obsessively searched for any report of a body found in her old neighborhood. She finally found it: a small, buried article about an unidentified male discovered with a severe head injury in a Mahim apartment. He had been taken to a public hospital, where he had slipped into a coma. Then, a week later, he had simply disappeared from his bed—another ghost swallowed by the city's indifferent machinery, his case file stamped and forgotten. The ghost in her apartment was gone. For the first time since the night the sky fell, Chung could finally, truly, breathe.

Vikrant's end was messier, a collection of sordid, conflicting rumors that drifted back to Sujata like smoke through the open door of her own café. She overheard them from the gossip of the local delivery boys and the whispers of old acquaintances who still worked the bars. One story claimed he'd fled to Delhi after getting on the wrong side of a powerful loan shark. Another, more brutal tale, said he'd picked a fight in a drunken stupor in a dive bar and ended up with a broken neck. A third, the one Sujata quietly believed the most, was that he had simply moved on, a predator seeking new hunting grounds, finding some other city, some other desperate girl to torment. She never asked for details. She didn't need the grim closure of knowing his exact fate. All the closure she needed was the sound of Anaya's easy, healthy laughter as she did her homework at the corner table, a sound that filled every dusty, sunlit corner of the small kingdom they had built. The world that had tried so hard to break them had blinked, and in that single moment of distraction, they had won.

Full Circle

The idea, when it came, was Dev's. They were sitting on overturned plastic crates outside the now-shuttered Scarlet Café, basking in the relative quiet of the late evening. The air was thick with the smell of night-blooming jasmine and the ever-present perfume of diesel fumes. Dev, who had been idly flipping a bottle cap across the cracked pavement, finally spoke into the comfortable silence. "We should take one last trip," he said, his voice quiet, almost hesitant. "Back to where it all started."

Rahul, who had been in the middle of a loud, passionate rant about a difficult client, fell instantly silent. He let out a low, noncommittal grunt, a rough sound that was a transparent attempt to hide a sudden, unexpected wave of emotion. Chung snorted, ever the cynic. "Getting sentimental in your old age, Wanderwolf?" she teased, though her voice lacked its usual bite.

Dev just shrugged, a small, easy smile playing on his lips. "Maybe," he said. "It's a full moon tonight. Just like it was then."

Sujata, who had been watching him with a soft, knowing expression, smiled. It was a smile that held more weight and understanding than any words could. She tucked a stray strand of hair behind her ear. "When do we leave?" she asked, her voice a quiet confirmation.

"Tonight," Dev said simply.

And so they went. Their procession was a chaotic, joyful, and utterly ridiculous mess. Dev and Sujata led the way on his still-battered Honda. Rahul and Chung followed, crammed into the back of a sputtering auto-rickshaw they'd haggled for, its ancient engine groaning in protest. From a cheap Bluetooth speaker, a playlist of scratchy, old Bollywood classics blasted into the night, the terrible music a perfect soundtrack to their imperfect victory. They laughed and shouted jokes at each other over the noise as the city peeled away behind them—the glittering, arrogant towers giving way to the humble, sleeping chawls, which in turn bled into the dark, skeletal remains of the factories at the city's edge.

They found the old textile estate just after midnight, the entire, forgotten landscape bathed in the cool, silver light of the full moon. The place was transformed. The raw, smoking, angry wound in the earth was gone, completely healed over by three months of the city's stubborn, wild, and irrepressible growth. Weeds and even a few determined wildflowers now grew in a thick, soft carpet over the site. But if you knew exactly where to look, if you knew the secret language of the land, you could still see it—a faint, shallow depression in the earth, a subtle, almost imperceptible scar. And if you squinted just right, you could almost imagine the faint, ghostly shimmer of stardust still buried deep beneath the new, green roots.

They stood in a quiet circle at the edge of what had once been the crater, the terrible music from the speaker now mercifully silenced. There were no sirens here. There was no fear. There was only the quiet, living hum of the night and the shared, unspoken memory of the four desperate, broken people who had died in this field and the four new ones who had been born from its ashes.

Rahul broke the comfortable silence by pulling an old, dented flask of cheap rum from his pocket and tossing it gently into the center of their circle. "To the ghosts," he said, his voice more serious than he intended.

Chung laughed, a surprisingly beautiful, rusty sound in the quiet night. She picked it up, took a long, unapologetic swig that made Rahul's eyes water just watching, and passed it to Sujata. Sujata took a small, delicate sip and passed it to Dev, who did the same before passing it back to Rahul. They sat in the tall, wild grass, cross-legged and content, passing the flask and their old ghosts back and forth in the moonlight until neither felt quite so heavy anymore.

"I used to think we were cursed," Sujata said suddenly, her voice a quiet murmur. She was plucking the petals from a wildflower, her movements slow and thoughtful. "I thought this city picked us, specifically, to break. That we were all born with targets on our backs." She looked up then, her gaze moving from one beloved, familiar face to the next. "But looking at you all now... maybe we weren't cursed. Maybe we were just being prepared."

"Prepared for what?" Rahul asked, his voice rough with emotion.

Sujata smiled, a small, steady, certain expression that seemed to radiate a light of its own. "For each other."

The words settled in the quiet field, heavy and beautiful and true. Dev, emboldened by the rum and the moment, shifted closer to her, his fingers gently brushing against hers. It wasn't a demand; it was a quiet, hopeful question. She answered by twining her pinky finger with his, a small, brave, and definite yes. Across the circle, Rahul cleared his throat loudly, suddenly finding the scuffed toe of his shoe to be the most fascinating thing in the world. Chung rolled her eyes and tossed a small pebble that bounced harmlessly off his knee. "Don't get mushy, Uncle." He just laughed, a deep, easy sound that was no longer a stranger to him.

Before they left, they stood, drawn by an unspoken need, in the center of the faint depression in the earth, the place where the sky had once touched the ground. No one suggested it. They just did it. Dev held out his hand, palm up. Sujata placed hers on top of his. Rahul added his, his hand steady and sure. Chung slapped hers down last, a defiant sound in the quiet night. It wasn't a promise to be rich or to be safe. It was a silent, unbreakable promise to always find their way back. Back to this spot. Back to each other.

Finally, with a shared, unspoken agreement, they each kicked a small bit of dirt over the ground where the ghost gold still shimmered. It wasn't an act of hiding a secret but of burying a memory. The miracle from the sky had brought them together, but the family they had built, they had built with their own two scarred hands. As they drove back into the hungry, roaring mouth of the city, they were not afraid. They had fallen, and for the first time in their lives, they knew, with absolute and unshakable certainty, that there would always be someone there to catch them.

CHAPTER TWENTY

THE STARS WE KEPT

Five years later, Mumbai was a city of new scars and shinier, more expensive skin. Gleaming glass towers clawed at the smoggy sky where old mills used to stand, and elevated metro lines sliced through neighborhoods that had once been tangled, slow, and knowable. But underneath the relentless ambition and the new, hungry money, the city's heart was the same: dusty, defiant, and stubbornly, chaotically alive.

Tucked in a stubborn little lane off a crowded main road, squeezed between two glittering mobile shops that flashed violent red and yellow signs, **Scarlet Café** had also survived. It hadn't grown bigger. It hadn't gotten fancier. It had simply endured, a small, warm, and utterly immovable anchor in the city's churning sea. The chalkboard outside still read, in Sujata's neat script, *"Today's Special: Hope and Cutting Chai—INR 20."*

Inside, the air was a warm, fragrant cloud of brewing cardamom, frying onions, and a happiness so palpable it felt like another ingredient. Anaya, now a vibrant, radiant teenager with a laugh that was far too loud for the small space, navigated the crowded tables with the easy grace of a performer, a tray of steaming vada pavs balanced perfectly on one hand. Behind the counter, Sujata moved with the calm, easy rhythm of a queen in her own, beloved kingdom. She paused to wink at Dev, who was perched precariously on a stepladder, wrestling with a jammed and belligerent ceiling fan. He was still stubborn, and his old limp still returned on rainy days, but the love between them was now a quiet, settled thing, a constant presence as warm and comforting as the chai she was brewing.

Across the city, on the fifth floor of a crumbling industrial block in Andheri, **Starfall Couriers Pvt. Ltd.** was a symphony of glorious, controlled chaos. Dozens of battered bikes leaned in chaotic rows against the loading dock, and two dented but proud Tata Ace trucks waited to be loaded. Inside the tiny, crowded office, delivery boys—some barely older than Anaya—shouted across the room in a joyful, messy mix of Marathi, Hindi, and English.

At the heart of the beautiful chaos, in a glass cabin no bigger than a closet, sat Rahul. His hair was streaked with more grey now, the lines on his face were deeper, but his eyes were bright, alight with the fierce, hungry energy of a man building an empire one parcel at a time. He paused from flipping through invoices to check his phone, a fond, foolish smile spreading across his face. The lock screen was a photo of Chung. She was grinning wildly at the camera, a scratched-up electric guitar slung across her back, a chubby toddler with a fistful of her hair perched on her hip, both of them giving the camera a defiant peace sign. He played the last voice note she'd sent him in the middle of the night: *"Hey, Uncle Starfall. A kid named Surya just nailed his first solo. You'd cry, trust me."* She was still running **The Dreamer's Den**, still teaching dirty-faced kids how to make a beautiful, angry noise, still his partner in a different, quieter kind of survival. Rahul watched the scene before him: Dev perched precariously on a stepladder, Sujata winking at him from behind the counter, Anaya navigating the tables with a performer's grace. He listened to the happy, chaotic din of the café and the distant, familiar roar of his own delivery bikes hitting the streets. He checked his phone, a fond, foolish smile spreading across his face at a new photo from Chung—a dirty-faced kid grinning wildly, holding a beat-up guitar like it was a holy relic. This was it. Not a dream, not a fantasy, but a noisy, messy, and gloriously real life, forged from the dust of a fallen star.

Tonight was one of those nights. It wasn't spoken of, and it wasn't scheduled in any calendar. It was a pull, an unspoken, magnetic understanding that after a long, hard week of battling the city, they needed to find their way back to their center.

In the warm, fragrant kitchen of Scarlet Café, Dev slid the heavy, groaning shutter down, the familiar sound signaling the end of the day. The last customer had just left, and Sujata was already at work, her movements a familiar, comforting dance. She filled a large steel flask with her best, sweet, and heavily spiced chai, its aroma filling the small space. Beside it, she wrapped a generous portion of leftover samosas in newspaper. Anaya, who had been finishing her homework at her usual corner table, saw the familiar ritual and grinned. Without a word, she grabbed her battered ukulele from its hook on the wall and gave Dev a conspiratorial wink. It was time.

Across town, Rahul stood at the loading dock of Starfall Couriers, the air thick with the smell of petrol and the satisfying chaos of a day's work done. He barked half-serious threats at his last few delivery boys as they prepared to head home. "I hear one scratch on that bike tomorrow, and it's coming out of your pay!" he yelled over the roar of an engine. "Unless you crashed it for love, or maybe for a very good pizza. Then we can talk." The boys laughed, giving him a mock salute as they sped off into the night.

In the noisy, beautiful chaos of The Dreamer's Den in Mahim, Chung handed two of her oldest, most trusted teenage students a crumpled five-hundred-rupee note. "Make sure the little ones don't burn the place down," she said, her version of a heartfelt babysitting instruction. "There are chips in the back. Do not, under any circumstances, touch my amp settings."

One by one, from different corners of the city, they converged. Their separate journeys, each a testament to a life rebuilt, pulled them toward a single, invisible point on the city's vast, chaotic map. They met near the highway, a strange and wonderful collection of bikes and a borrowed, sputtering auto-rickshaw, and began their pilgrimage. As the auto-rickshaw sputtered to a halt, Rahul heard it again: that same rhythmic, hollow thrum-thud from a nearby flyover. Years ago, it had sounded like a countdown to an ending. Now, it felt like the steady pulse of a city that had finally let them in. It was a noisy, joyful procession, so different from the silent, terrified flight they had made five years before. They were moving not away from danger, but toward a memory, toward the concrete heart of their shared history. They were going to the overpass, the place where everything had almost ended and, so, had truly begun.

They spread a ratty, faded bedsheet over the cracked asphalt, creating a small, clean island in the urban decay. They sat cross-legged, passing around warm beers wrapped in newspaper and the bag of now-cold samosas. The laughter started, loud and easy, echoing in the concrete hollow of the overpass, a sound of pure, unburdened joy.

Anaya, her face lit with happiness, began to strum her ukulele, launching into a clumsy, enthusiastic rendition of an old, romantic film song. Dev, full of more confidence than talent, immediately joined in, his loud, off-key singing so earnest and heartfelt that it sent Anaya into a fit of helpless giggles.

"You're ruining my art!" she shrieked, laughing so hard she could barely play.

"He can't ruin what's already broken," Chung deadpanned, without looking up from the beer bottle cap she was methodically trying to bend in half with her bare fingers.

Later, Rahul, gesturing passionately with a half-eaten samosa, launched into one of his favorite absurd theories. "I'm telling you," he argued to the group, "the auto drivers are the last true philosophers in this city. They see everything. They know everything. You can learn more about life in a fifteen-minute ride from Bandra to Juhu than in four years of university."

"I'll bet you ten rupees a street astrologer tells you the same thing next week and sells you a fake gemstone to 'improve your business karma,'" Chung retorted instantly, and Dev roared with a deep, full-throated laugh.

In the midst of the happy, comfortable chaos, Sujata leaned her head against Dev's shoulder. It was a small, quiet, and simple movement, but for her, it was everything. It was the feeling of a long, desperate, and terrifying journey finally ending. It was the feeling of being, finally and unshakably, home. He didn't tense or react; he simply relaxed into the touch, a silent, shared acknowledgment of their hard-won peace.

Eventually, the stories and the bad singing and the ridiculous arguments wound down. The last samosa was eaten. The last beer was finished. And a comfortable, profound silence settled over them, a quiet so full of love and shared history that it had no need for words. Above them, a few stubborn, miraculous stars managed to push through the city's hazy, yellow glow. They didn't need the glittering dust that was still buried in the field miles away. They didn't need any more miracles to fall from the sky. They had taken the one they were given and, with their own scarred and broken hands, had forged it into this. Into family. And against every brutal, crushing odd the city had thrown at them, it was more than enough.

The night deepened around them, wrapping them in a soft, familiar blanket. The distant pulse of the city was a constant, living thing—the mournful screech of a train, the impatient honk of a cab, and the faint, tinny melody of a radio from a faraway window. It was the ugly, beautiful, endless heartbeat of Mumbai, and for the first time, it sounded less like a threat and more like a lullaby.

They sat in their loose circle on the faded bedsheet, amidst the last of the samosa crumbs and the warm dregs of beer. No one felt the need to fill the silence. Anaya was lying on her back, her head in Sujata's lap, staring up at the few stubborn stars visible through the haze. Her fingers drifted across the strings of her ukulele, the cheap instrument buzzing softly. Then, her voice, clear and soft, cut through the quiet.

"Hum rahe ya na rahe, yaad aayenge yeh pal..."

The words—*whether we stay or not, these moments will be remembered*—floated into the night. Sujata's hand, which had been gently stroking Anaya's hair, stilled. Dev, who had been leaning back with a goofy, contented smile, closed his eyes, savoring the sound. Chung, who had been methodically trying to bend a bottle cap in half, paused, her fingers motionless. And Rahul, who had been sketching meaningless patterns on the concrete with a piece of chalk, looked up, his gaze soft. The simple, heartfelt song was a testament to everything they had fought for, a perfect, fragile note of peace in a world that had given them none.

It was Sujata who finally spoke into the comfortable quiet, her voice so low it was almost carried away by the thrum of the highway above. "I was just thinking," she began, her gaze fixed on a distant point in the darkness. "That night, at the crater... I think we buried the wrong thing."

The others turned to her, their curiosity piqued. She looked at them, a small, sad, and fiercely beautiful smile on her face. "We thought we were burying the last of the gold, putting the secret to rest. But that's not what happened. We were burying our fear. That was the moment we finally gave ourselves permission to want more than just survival."

A quiet, profound stillness settled over the group. Rahul stopped sketching, the piece of chalk held motionless in his hand. Chung's fingers stilled their restless play with the bottle cap. Dev nudged a small pebble with the toe of his boot, his entire focus on Sujata's words.

Anaya, who had been listening intently, sat up straight, hugging her ukulele to her chest. "I wasn't there," she said, her voice small but clear. "But I don't think you ever stopped." She looked from one face to the next, at their tired, scarred, and beloved features. "You're all still so brave. Every day. When Rahul-uncle argues on the phone, he sounds so loud, like a hero. And when Chung-aunty teaches the kids to make noise, they look so happy. And every morning, even when you're tired, you always open the café, Aunty Su."

The truth of her words, so simple and so profound, struck them all at once. A sound started in Dev's chest, a low rumble that wasn't a cough or a sob. It was a laugh. A rough, warm, broken sound of pure, unadulterated release. A moment later, Rahul joined in, then Sujata, and finally, even Chung. It was the kind of laughter that doesn't come from a joke but from a deep, shared, and finally healed wound.

Chung raised her empty beer bottle. "To still burying fear," she said, her voice completely serious.

They all followed, a clumsy, perfect chorus. Dev lifted the empty chai thermos with a solemn nod. Rahul gave a mock salute with his piece of chalk. Sujata held up Anaya's small ukulele like it was a sacred trophy. And Anaya, beaming, held up both hands in a V-for-victory sign.

"To always finding each other," she added, her voice bright with a certainty that anchored them all.

They sat like that for a long time, four broken kids who had finally, painfully, grown up, stitched together by something far stronger than luck or gold. They were a family. Not one made of blood, but the stronger kind, the kind made by choice. Eventually, reluctantly, they began the slow ritual of packing up. Anaya slung the ukulele over her back. Dev gathered the empty bottles into a bag. Rahul carefully crushed the last of the wrappers into a ball. Chung folded the old bedsheet into a neat, worn square.

Before they left, they gathered one last time in a tight, silent circle. There were no grand speeches. There were no tears. There was only a profound, unspoken knowing.

Dev reached out first, laying his calloused hand flat, palm up. Sujata placed her hand on top of his, her own scarred skin a testament to the battles she had won. Rahul added his, his grip steady and sure, the hand of a man who now built things instead of just enduring them. Chung slapped hers down with a defiant, grinning slap, a sound of a fight that had been won but was never forgotten. Finally, Anaya squeezed her small hand in on top of the pile, her young fingers a bridge to the future they had all fought for. One single, shared heartbeat. Five hearts stacked together against the sprawling, impossible city. They didn't need to say "forever." Some promises are too big for words.

They turned and walked away from the overpass without looking back. The stars they had buried years ago were not gone; they were burning inside their own bones now. They were not the desperate kids who had clawed gold from a smoking crater. They were the architects who had clawed hope from an indifferent universe. And they had won.

They walked back into the beautiful, ugly, endless chaos of Mumbai, back into the traffic and the smog, their laughter and their bickering a familiar music against the city's roar. They carried the quiet of this night inside them, a shared and sacred secret. They now understood the truth of their beginning. When the sky fell, it hadn't fallen to kill them. It had fallen to remind them that some things—hope, family, and a stubborn, defiant love—can survive anything. Even a city like Mumbai. Especially a city like Mumbai.

The End
Where the sky fell and we rose...

About The Author

Shiv Bhowmik

Shiv Bhowmik is a writer who crafts stories the way others live memories—through silence, ache, and revelation. A data analyst by profession and a storyteller by becoming, Shiv's work is a meditation on the unspoken: survival, connection, and the fragile beauty of remembering.

His relationship with writing wasn't sparked by passion but nurtured like trust—patiently, in solitude. Each of his works is a fragment of feeling, a quiet reckoning. He writes not to explain, but to evoke. Not to escape the moment, but to deepen it.

His fiction explores the beauty in broken people, the silence between words, and the fierce hope that lingers after survival. **When the Sky Fell Gold** is his cinematic, emotionally layered take on what it means to be left behind—and to rise anyway.

More About The Author

Stay connected with Shiv: You'll find more of his words, worlds, and reflections here:
YouTube | Instagram | Threads | X (formerly Twitter)
@shiv_bhowmik

Notes